A BLESSED DREAM

BRIDES OF BLESSINGS BOOK 8

DANICA FAVORITE

For anyone who has ever had a dream.

PROLOGUE

S pring 1852
     Central Valley, California

TONIGHT WOULD BE THE MONTGOMERY SISTERS' last night in the only home they'd ever known. But that didn't mean they had any idea what they were going to do next. The sheriff was coming tomorrow. They'd already been warned. Louisa stared at the pages of a book she'd read nearly a hundred times. None of the words made sense. Perhaps it was because the sound of her sisters arguing over their plans made it nearly impossible.

"Would you please put down that book and tell Thomasina she's being foolish?"

Josephine's voice had reached a level of shrillness one simply could not ignore. Louisa didn't want to ignore her sister, but she also didn't want to get caught in the middle of another one of their arguments.

She closed her book and set it inside her carpet bag. They

had each packed a trunk and a small suitcase to take with them to their new home, wherever that was. It seemed ridiculous to think they'd be able to take all their belongings with them, not when there was nowhere to go. Their neighbor, Isaac Barnes, had offered to take them in, but his ranch was just as small and struggling as theirs had been. Rumor had it that the bank would be taking his place very soon. After all, their father had lent him money to stay afloat already. On one hand, she appreciated her father's charitable works. On the other hand, it did them little good now that he was gone.

Murdered and robbed on his way home from the sale of their cattle, it seemed that every sacrifice their father had made, for family and neighbor, had been absolutely futile. There would have been enough money to pay the mortgage had he returned home safely. There would have been enough money to do a lot of things, but now it was gone.

Josephine gave Louisa a pleading look. "Tell Thomasina that we will go to Isaac's. He's promised us a home, and we can help him on his ranch, so he can get back on his feet. When he does, he's promised us that he will pay back the money Father lent him, and then we can have a place of our very own."

Louisa knew the source of Josephine's tears wasn't so much the thought of the unknown, but the thought of leaving behind her precious animals. If they went to town, and used their meager savings on a hotel, there would be no place to keep the animals.

"Josephine does have a point," Louisa said. "What will we do when the money runs out? We can afford a hotel for a month, maybe two. Will that be long enough for us to find jobs? I applied for the schoolteacher position, but they filled it with some man who'd gone to college. I can't compete against that."

She did her best to hide her frustration, considering the past few weeks had been nothing but a series of disappointments for the sisters. They all had lost so much more than their father. Not just the teaching job stolen out from under Louisa. Thomasina's fiancé had rejected her after realizing the truth about her disfigurement. And Josephine's prized mare had given birth to a stillborn foal. Everything the girls had ever loved was taken from them in just a few short weeks.

"Maybe we shouldn't stay in town," Thomasina said. "I'm a laughingstock, because Edward made it known to everyone that I am not a normal woman."

Her sister's face mottled red with anger. Louisa reached forward and took her sister's hands. "You are a real woman. The doctor said so. He can't explain why you're different, but we certainly do not see you as being defective in any way. Perhaps Edward's rejection of you was more about the loss of potential fortune than your appearance."

Thomasina jerked her hand away. "I have a beard. If I don't shave twice daily, then it's obvious to all. What man wants a wife who shaves more than he does? I'm a monstrosity, that's what they all say. And maybe they're right. Who could love a woman like me?"

A lot of people, if they got to know Thomasina's generous and loving heart. But if she told her sister that a thousand times, Thomasina would have denied it a thousand and one. It did them no good to have this argument.

"One of us should marry," Josephine said. "I know we all agreed to marry only for love, but perhaps if one of us could find a husband, he would provide for us, and then we wouldn't have to leave. I'm sure, in time, people will forget your scandal."

Thomasina glared at her younger sister. "And just who might you marry? The blacksmith's son, who used to chase you with snakes? Or perhaps Harold Larson. He must be nigh on sixty, but I hear he needs someone to raise his children from the three wives he buried in succession. Perhaps you'd like to be the fourth."

Josephine didn't respond, and really, there wasn't a response. There were no marriageable men, at least not any decent ones, anywhere in town. Josephine's only reason for staying was the animals.

A knock at the door interrupted the discussion.

"I can't see anyone like this," Thomasina said. She turned and went into the bedroom. She hadn't shaved that evening, and anyone who looked at her closely could see the stubble. It was a surprise visit like this one that had scared off her fiancé.

Louisa got up and opened the door. The sheriff stood staring back at her.

"You aren't due until tomorrow. Surely you aren't throwing us out in the middle of the night. We deserve at least one more night in our own beds."

Sheriff Boyd at least had the decency to look chagrined. "You know I hate doing this. I've known you since you were babies. Your father and I grew up together. But the bank is forcing my hand."

Even if he did feel bad, it didn't excuse him intruding on their last night in their home.

"We have until tomorrow," she said firmly.

"That's not why I'm here. The sheriff from the town where your father was found sent over some of his personal effects. They're not much, but I thought you might like to have them."

He held out a parcel that felt so light, it hardly seemed worth the trouble. But he was right. They were grateful for it.

"Thank you. I hope you won't think us too rude if we ask you to leave now. We want to enjoy every moment we can before we must leave this place we've grown to love so much."

He gave a jerky nod. "I did my best to buy you more time, I hope you know that."

What did it matter? A day, a week, it still meant leaving the only home they've ever known.

"Thank you. I'd like to get back to my sisters."

As soon as Louisa closed the door behind the sheriff, Thomasina stepped out of her room. "Personal effects? I thought the robbers had taken everything when they killed our father."

"Including his horses," Josephine mumbled.

Louisa brought the package to the table and opened it. Their father's favorite shirt. His pants. His belt, missing the prized silver buckle. And his boots.

"This must have been what he was wearing when he died," Thomasina said. "I assumed they'd buried him in them."

Louisa shook her head. "My understanding was they were going to try to sell his remaining clothing to pay for the grave. I'm surprised they've sent it back to us. I guess they couldn't get anything for these measly items, so they decided to let us have them."

At least that's what had been explained to her by the man who'd brought them the news initially. Sad to think that in the end, this was all Father had left. And it was found to be worthless.

Tears filled Josephine's eyes. "I hate to think of him, lying in a cold grave, without even his clothes to keep him warm. He always said he wanted to be buried by Mother."

"Maybe someday we can afford to have his remains moved. But there wasn't money to bring his body home, and we made the best arrangements we could at the time." Thomasina's voice was firm, resolute. The undertaker had wanted a small fortune to send her father's body home. Money they didn't have.

"I'm glad to have his things," Thomasina said. She took his shirt and held it against her. "It still smells like him, even though he's been gone for months."

But then she dropped it. Louisa reached for the shirt, and in doing so, saw why her sister had so quickly dropped the shirt.

It was splattered with bloodstains.

"He was killed in this." Josephine said. "Why would anyone think we would want it?"

"Because it's the last thing we have of him," Thomasina said. "Look at how plain his clothes are. Why would anyone assume he had money and murder him for it?"

They were just old work clothes. But obviously whoever had killed him had searched him thoroughly enough to steal anything of value, including his belt buckle. Whoever killed their father was an evil, horrible person.

Thomasina picked up his pants, bringing them to her nose. "They smell like him, too."

She held them up to the light, examining them. "I don't believe these have any of his blood. Perhaps I could make pillows out of them, one for each of us, as something to remember him by."

Josephine stood. "As if we would forget."

Tears rolled down Josephine's face as she stared at the meager pile. "This still doesn't solve what we're going to do."

As Thomasina folded the pants, a strange look crossed her face. "There's something in his pockets."

She dug into them and found a piece of paper.

"A blacksmith receipt. From a place called Blessings.

That's not where father took the cattle. What was he doing there?"

Louisa remembered reading something in the paper about a town called Blessings up north. "It's another town with gold. Father once spoke about wanting to try his hand at finding a golden nugget."

"He would never leave the ranch," Josephine said. "He loves this place."

"It was heavily mortgaged," Thomasina said. "He once said that he thought he could get more money selling the cattle to mining camps for meat than if he took them to San Francisco. Perhaps that's what he did."

None of it made sense. "But he was murdered in a town outside San Francisco," Louisa said. "And the gold mines are quite a distance from there. What was he doing so far away?"

Thomasina studied the receipt. "It just says for services rendered. What services?"

She flipped the receipt over. "Winslet? What does that mean?"

The girls all looked at each other. If he'd wanted to sell his cattle in Blessings, wouldn't he have been killed there? The deputy who'd come to notify them of their father's death had told them that he had sold the cattle to his usual operation outside of San Francisco and was headed out of town when he was murdered and robbed. He told them that it was unlikely they'd ever find the culprit, as such things were common. Other than the fact that his trip had taken longer than usual, they'd had no reason to believe there was anything different about this one, other than his murder.

But finding out that he'd gone someplace else, to a different town? That changed things.

How, Louisa didn't know. But it seemed mighty strange.

"This doesn't add up," Thomasina said. "He'd never run

into trouble on his cattle runs before. Why would this would be different?"

Louisa nodded. "I was thinking the same thing. Do you think the side trip to Blessings has anything to do with it?"

"If the authorities can't solve his murder, then why would we think we can? We're better off figuring out what we're going to do tomorrow rather than speculating about something that has no bearing on our future," Josephine said.

Thomasina banged on the table. "It's never sat right with me that Father's murderer has gotten away with it. Who will he murder next? What other family is going to be in our position because of this horrible person? We owe it to him to find out the truth."

"And how do you suppose we do that?" Josephine crossed her arms across her chest.

"We're going to Blessings," Thomasina said. "I want to know what Father was doing there. Whatever it was, it might have been what got him killed."

Louisa's skin bristled with excitement. Her sister's idea gave them somewhere to go and something to do. And yet...

"We're three women, without the protection of a man. No one's going to take us seriously," Louisa pointed out. "The bank ran us right out of the building when we proposed running the ranch ourselves." It wasn't that she disliked the plan, but they'd already faced humiliation for being three women on their own.

Thomasina rubbed her chin. "True, but if the sisters had an older brother, they would take the brother seriously."

Louisa laughed. "If only we had such a brother. It's why we have boys' names, because Father wanted a son so desperately."

"I'll be the brother." Thomasina ran her fingers along her cheek. "If we leave tomorrow, by the time we reach Blessings, I'll have a full beard. Everyone will think I'm a man. We'll tell them I'm your brother, and because I'm a man, I'll have access to people and places you don't. We can find out what happened to our father."

Josephine frowned. "And if his time in Blessings has nothing to do with his death?"

"Then we'll move on. But we owe it to him to try to find out." Thomasina's voice was firm.

Josephine didn't budge. "We have no money."

Did it matter? No matter where they went, they had no money. But just like Thomasina didn't want to remain in the town where she'd faced humiliation, Louisa didn't want to face the people who'd rejected her for her dream job. There was nothing left for them here.

Louisa looked at her sister. "We have enough to live in the hotel for a few months. We can use that money for traveling expenses, and when we get to Blessings, we can find jobs."

Her words didn't wipe the stubborn expression from Josephine's face. "How are we supposed to do that, when no one here will hire us?"

Thomasina gave them all a firm look. "They won't hire three sisters. But in a mining town, there's plenty of work for a man. I've helped Father run this ranch better than any of his hands. I can do any work that's available. And with an older brother as your protector, more jobs will be open to you."

The idea of Thomasina having to portray a man seemed almost ludicrous, except that Louisa could already see her sister's stubble growing back, and she remembered the time when Thomasina had been ill and had spent several days in bed. No one, other than Louisa and Josephine, had been allowed to see her, because by the time Thomasina was well, she did, in fact, have a full beard. With the beard, dressed in man's clothes, she just might be able to pull it off.

And as for the job opportunities, Thomasina was right.

With an older brother to vouch for them, people were less likely to make assumptions about the girls. When they'd asked around town about employment, some of the people had snickered and made the suggestion that perhaps the only profession available to them was the world's oldest. Apparently, three young ladies on their own weren't qualified for anything else.

"I think we should do it," Louisa said. "It would be better to be someplace where people don't know us and our tragedy. And I haven't been comfortable with the idea of relying on Isaac's charity. I know he means well, but with unmarried women living with a widower, people will talk."

"What about the animals?" Josephine's voice wavered, and Louisa could tell she was fighting back tears.

"We can take the horses, because we'll need them for the wagon. I suppose we can find a way to bring some of the chickens. They'll be useful, as long as we can find a place where we can keep them."

"Our cat could be useful, to keep away mice. And the dog, for protection." Desperation filled Josephine's voice.

"As long as you can keep them contained in the wagon," Thomasina said. "Now that we know we'll be setting up household elsewhere, we should rethink what we've packed, and what will be useful in our new home. We'll be like all the other pioneers in search of a new life. We couldn't do so as women, but as two women and a brother, there are more opportunities available to us."

The sadness in Thomasina's voice made Louisa's heart hurt. Of all the sisters, she most liked having pretty things, and was, ironically, the most feminine. But her figure had never been conducive to the gowns she so loved. She'd hated the teasing that had come when people found out about her beard. Being called a freak. And once, in town, a group of boys had lifted her skirts to see if she had other manly features.

Thomasina had suffered the most humiliation at her affliction and Louisa would have never asked her to pretend to be a man. Except it had been Thomasina's idea to use it to their advantage, so Louisa would support her sister in that.

"So, we're going to Blessings?" Louisa looked at her sisters. "I think, out of all of our options, it's the best."

Josephine nodded slowly. "I hate to admit it, but you're right. I don't like how Isaac treats his animals, and he often mocks me for acting like they're our pets. I've been afraid that one of our chickens will end up in his stew pot."

Her sister's notorious devotion to their animals, particularly the chickens, was another reason folks here liked to laugh at them. Their father had indulged her, saying it didn't matter as long as she didn't decide that one of his prized cattle was a pet. Louisa smiled at the memory. How she missed him.

"It's settled then." Thomasina stood. "I'll go through father's things to see what I can use to transform me. We'll have to repack our trunks with the idea that we'll have to set up a completely new household. I don't know how much of our furniture we can fit in the wagon, but at least now, we can bring some of our treasured belongings."

She pulled the pins out of her hair. As her long, silky locks tumbled down her back, she sighed. "I don't want the townspeople to give us away, so once we've gone far enough that we won't be recognized, will find a place where I can sell my hair. After that, I'll let my beard grow, and I will become Tom."

The girls used to joke about being Tom, Lou and Joe, the boys their father never had. And now, in death, he'd finally have one. Louisa hoped that the murderer would be caught soon, so Thomasina wouldn't have to live like this forever. She deserved happiness just as much as any of them.

And maybe, in a town with a name like Blessings, the good Lord would finally show up in their lives and send a few their way. It seemed like God had turned his back on them the day their father died, and though she'd prayed daily for a miracle, they'd been given nothing. Could Blessings be the answer to their prayers?

CHAPTER 1

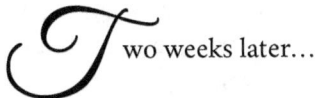wo weeks later…

THEY HAD BARELY ARRIVED in Blessings when they quickly discovered who this Winslet written on the back of the receipt was: Atherton Winslet, founder of Blessings.

Staring at the wiry old man, Louisa couldn't help thinking that coming here had been a waste of their time. Not only was this man obviously incapable of hurting a fly, he also seemed equally incapable of plotting something so heinous as her father's murder.

But she didn't know she could trust him, either.

Looking around the dusty streets, she couldn't understand what had brought her father here. He'd gone out of his way to stop here on what should have been a simple trip to San Francisco. It didn't make sense to go days out of his way to visit a blacksmith, when he could have stopped at any number of towns in between.

The blacksmith, George Willis, had said the receipt was

for something simple, like a horseshoe, but he couldn't remember anything more. Of course, he'd been so drunk that he could barely stand, so they wouldn't be able to trust what he said anyway. Tom hadn't wanted to press the man, so here they were, talking to the only other person who might know something about their father.

"Do you know of a house to rent? A place for me and my sisters to stay? And anyone who might be hiring?" Tom's questions came out rapidly. She'd practiced lowering her voice during their journey, and now, she sounded just like a man.

Surely she didn't intend for them to stay long-term? There didn't seem to be very much here. Sure, it had all the makings of a growing town, with various buildings going up, and different shops along the main street, but as Louisa looked around at the rough people walking the streets, it lacked a certain refinement to it that didn't seem to be a welcoming place for women and children.

And as Mr. Winslet looked over at them, she couldn't help thinking that he agreed. Even though they'd come from a ranch, and weren't dressed in their finery, they definitely looked out of place here.

But then Mr. Winslet glanced at their wagon. "You folks look like you're hoping to settle here."

They'd loaded their wagon with everything they could take from the house, probably a little too much, and there were times when she thought she wasn't sure they'd get over the pass. But they'd made it. Tom had driven the wagon, and Louisa and Josephine had ridden in on Josephine's prized mares. It was a shame their father's stallion had been taken when he'd been killed, because he had been the key to all of Josephine's horse breeding dreams.

Tied to the back of the wagon were two of their cows. The others they'd had to sell to pay the bills, but she'd insisted in keeping at least those two, which were all they could take, ponying them behind as they rode. Sitting on the driver seat, was their dog, Zeus, and curled up next to him was the old barn cat. And of course, tied up on the back of the wagon was a cage Josephine had made for her chickens.

To any observer, they did look as if they were looking for a permanent home.

Mr. Winslet scratched his head. "What are you planning on doing with all those animals of yours?"

"We had a ranch and we lost it," Tom said. "But we hope to someday have a new home, a new ranch, and my sister just couldn't part with these animals. I know it's a lot to ask, but is there a place for rent where we can keep them? Or perhaps another local rancher, where we could board them?"

It was strange, looking at her sister dressed like a man. But having been in disguise for over a week now, Tom looked less and less feminine every day. Her beard was so thick and full, no one would mistake her for a woman.

The sisters had also changed their last name, in case someone recognized Montgomery and it warned off their father's killer. They were now the Davidson sisters, since their father was David.

Mr. Winslet nodded slowly. "I had a couple of fellows who wanted to start a livery, but it only got half built before winter arrived, and they decided they couldn't abide the cold. Another outfit moved in, but they didn't like the property, so they built somewhere else. This place is only half finished, but if you're the industrious sort, it wouldn't take but a couple days' worth of work to make it habitable. Some of the fences may need repairing, but it'll hold animals for now."

A large woman, dressed in what must have once been fine clothes, but were now tattered and worn, pushed her way into the group. "How much for one of your chickens? It's been ages since we've had chicken, and we're having company later this week. A fine roast chicken dinner would be just the thing."

Josephine spun. "My chickens are not for sale. Nor are they for eating. You go on now, and you leave my chickens alone."

A gentleman, if one could call someone wearing similarly tattered clothing, shoved past the woman. "Miss, I'll double what she's offering." He reached for the cage.

Josephine whipped out her fan and smacked him on the knuckles with it. "Don't you touch my chickens. They aren't for sale. Get your own chickens."

The man and woman walked away slowly, the man shaking his head and muttering about foolish women. Josephine turned to Mr. Winslet. "Why does everyone want my chickens? Can't they get their own?"

Mr. Winslet chuckled. "It's impractical to bring chickens here. It's a difficult journey, and many don't survive. Plus, they take up too much space, space that can be used for many other goods. A man can bring over a couple chickens, or several pounds of flour and other staples. To the people of Blessings, chicken is a luxury."

Josephine shook her head. "Well, it's a luxury they will have to do without."

Mr. Winslet smiled at her. "What about eggs? Do you ever have any to spare?"

Josephine gave a small shrug. "I might."

"You'll find eggs are just as dear. Again, they're difficult to transport, so it's a rare thing for a person to have eggs. If you're ever willing to part with any, I know my wife would greatly appreciate it. She's a fine cook, and though she has managed to compensate, she would be mighty grateful to have some eggs."

Louisa liked the fact that Mr. Winslet addressed her sister, as if he knew that they deferred to her when it came to the animals. To Tom and Louisa, they were merely tools of the ranch, but to Josephine, they were so much more. Every animal, including the chickens, had names. Most of the time, Louisa couldn't tell the chickens apart. But Josephine could. Which was why she had no doubt of her sister's love for the animals and she'd protect Josephine's right to keep them.

Mr. Winslet turned his attention back to Tom. "What kind of work are you looking for?"

"I've been thinking of working in the mines. But any honest work will do. I've spent my whole life helping our father run our ranch. I'm not afraid of hard work."

Because Tom had been driving the wagon for over a week now, her hands had become rough and calloused, like those of a man who worked for a living. And it was a good thing, because that was the first place Mr. Winslet looked before answering Tom's question.

"I could put a word in for you at the mine. Lots of men willing, but you'll find the work isn't as easy as you think."

Tom nodded slowly. "I'm willing to give it a try. My sisters are also hoping to find jobs. Are there any respectable positions for a lady around here?"

Louisa liked her emphasis on "respectable." Of course, given Tom's disguise, they were probably throwing respectability right out the window. But at least they were doing their best. Once they solved their father's murder, and were able to shake off the ruse, Tom would re-establish her identity as a woman in a new town, in a new place, where no one knew them.

"I'm sure my sister would be delighted to share some of her eggs when we have some as a way of thanking you for helping us find jobs and accommodations," Tom said.

Mr. Winslet gave a warm smile. "That isn't necessary. I wouldn't want to upset your sister. I'm always happy to help people get settled in our town, especially fine folks like your-selves who intend to settle here."

None of them corrected him. Even though he didn't seem like the sort to have anything to do with her father's murder, one couldn't be too certain about strangers.

Mr. Winslet looked at Tom like he was trying to figure her out. "Are you sure you want to work in a mine?"

He couldn't possibly suspect that Tom was really a woman. Could he?

"I worked with our father from sunup to sundown. We built our ranch from nothing, and I drove in every post myself. I can handle the work."

That part wasn't a story. Their father had worked them just as hard as any boys. He'd needed the help. Tom had always been the biggest and strongest of them all.

"Very well," Mr. Winslet said. "I'll have a word with my manager. He's always looking for good help. If you're sure you're up to the task. As for the ladies, have you considered taking in wash? Our miners are always looking for someone to do the laundry."

Louisa had read about such things. It wasn't an easy job, doing laundry, but it was one she and her sisters knew well. She glanced over at Tom. Tom wouldn't be able to help them. They'd always counted on their elder sister to do much of the heavy lifting. But if Tom could do it, so could they.

"We're happy to," Louisa said. "We'd be glad for the work."

Josephine made a noise, like the last thing she wanted was to do laundry, and Louisa didn't blame her. None of them enjoyed doing laundry, but with Tom making such a great sacrifice for the family, how could they not? They had no other means to support themselves, and even if they weren't searching for their father's killer, they would still need to find a way to provide a roof over their heads.

"That settles it, then," Mr. Winslet said. "I'll show you to the place I had in mind. I'll warn you, it's not much, but, with a little hard work and ingenuity, I believe it will be perfect for your family to stay in until you can find a place of your own."

The property, situated near the river toward the end of town, wasn't much to look at. The house, if you could call it that, only had three walls. But as they got closer, Louisa realized that was probably what had passed for a barn. Behind it was a tiny little shack, with no windows, and no door, just an opening that she supposed someone secured by putting a piece of cloth over it as she'd seen in some of the towns they passed through. It had a rank smell, like some forlorn creature had died in there.

The one-room shack was littered with junk of all sorts. She didn't know what to make of any of it. Looking around the space, it was clear not all of their belongings would fit. She was still mentally calculating how each of them would be able to sleep, while allowing room for their trunks and a table and chairs.

"Now that I've brought you to see it, I can see that it may not do. The young ladies wouldn't have a separate space of their own and that wouldn't be proper. Not with, er, your brother."

He did suspect. He had to. Why else did calling Tom their brother give him such pause?

"I can assure you that I am their brother," Tom said. "I'm not trying to disguise an inappropriate relationship with women or planning to set them up as sporting girls or anything else untoward. I believe I made myself quite clear that they only wanted respectable employment, as they are young ladies, and have always been raised as such."

Mr. Winslet turned red. "I'm terribly sorry. I didn't mean it that way."

Tom looked around the place. "This will do for now.

Better than a tent, and it wouldn't be too difficult to add on a room."

She looked over at her sisters. "You remember how we helped Father build the extra room when we thought that..."

She hesitated, and Louisa's heart sank a little. Their mother had died in childbirth, hoping to finally give their father the son he'd always wanted, even though the doctor said they shouldn't have more children. The worst part was, that baby had also been a girl. But they had made a nice room, which meant they could do it again.

"I assume that building out there is to be the barn," Josephine said, sounding put out.

"As I said, I believe the original intention was to turn it into a livery. So, it's extra large, and will provide plenty of room. I realize it isn't quite what people coming from a ranch might be used to, but it will house your horses and your cows, and you can build a secure pen for your chickens."

Given there was a house on the other side of the barn, and another house on the other side of what she assumed to be the lot, this was all the space there was. But Mr. Winslet was right. For now, it would do.

"Once you folks get settled, we can talk to the land office about finding you some land farther out. We recently had a couple establish a ranch outside of town, and I'm sure they would be happy to share what they've learned about the area, and what might make a good place for a second ranch. You'll find most of the people here are quite cooperative and are always happy to lend a hand. We all want to see Blessings grow, and see it become a home we can be proud of."

Now she felt even worse for thinking that Mr. Winslet could possibly have anything to do with her father's murder. He seemed so nice, so helpful. She almost wanted to ask him if he remembered him. The sisters had agreed that it would be best for Tom to ask the questions, to say that he was looking into the murder of a neighbor. None of them knew what their father might have said to anyone else. But he was quite proud of his daughters, and always looking to make a match for them. Anyone who knew their father would see through their ruse.

Zeus barked, and they exited the small house to see what was going on. A little boy and a little girl had stepped into the yard. Zeus didn't like strangers, and that was one of the reasons why they brought him with them. He would be good for keeping watch in such a strange place. Their father had purchased him for that very reason, wanting to know his daughters would be safe when he was out of town.

"Hello," Louisa said. "We're going to be moving in here. Do you live nearby?"

The little boy turned and hid his face against his sister. But the girl nodded. "Right there." She pointed at the house next door.

"My pa was hoping to buy this place so he can use the shed as his workshop." The little girl sent a glare in Mr. Winslet's direction. "You promised."

Mr. Winslet let out a long sigh. "It's only temporary. These fine folks are looking to settle here and need a larger piece of land for the animals. But this will give them a place to stay until they are able to find and build their ranch. I haven't broken my word to your father, and I certainly shall not."

A man stepped out of the house and started toward them. Even in the distance, there was a sadness to him, like he had had a great loss of his own. Something about him made Louisa want to put her arms around him and tell him that everything was going to be all right. A silly gesture, considering he was a stranger, and a man, therefore such an action would be inappropriate. But more than that, how could she promise him something like that when, some days, she didn't even know if that would be true for herself?

"Nathaniel. Callie. How many times have I told you not to play in the lot? It's not safe."

The little girl turned to him. "Mr. Winslet is here. He's letting some other people live here. But he promised it to us."

The man approached, taking off his hat, and running his fingers through his hair, making it look like a wild mess.

"It isn't your place to judge the actions of adults," he said. Then he approached Mr. Winslet.

JONAH HASTINGS WALKED over to them, forcing a pleasant smile on his face. Hopefully his children hadn't done something more terrible than speaking disrespectfully to adults. Why couldn't his sister keep an eye on them the way she'd promised?

He was doing his best to make a living for his family, and all he asked of Clarissa was that she care for them, protect them, and keep them out of trouble. Surely that wasn't too much to ask.

When his wife had died, Clarissa had come to stay with them, leaving her hated job at the dry goods store where she worked just outside of San Francisco.

It had seemed like a good idea and, at the time, Clarissa had gratefully accepted. But lately, she seemed more and more disinterested in caring for his children.

Jonah smiled pleasantly at Mr. Winslet. "So good to see you. What can we do for you?"

"We have a new family in our midst. And while I know you and I have been working out a deal for you to purchase this land and the building, it will be some time before you have the funds, and I'm offering it to them as a temporary home until they find a place suitable for their needs."

He gestured to a large wagon in the distance.

Jonah couldn't help gawking. When he'd first come to Blessings, he'd seen all sorts of wagons loaded with any number of oddities, but this one beat them all. The ordinary farm wagon was overloaded with furniture, boxes, and other personal belongings, as was common. But a scruffy dog and rather large cat sat on top of the pile all as if they were standing guard. If it were just the dog, he would think it normal, but the cat, right next to him, seemed out of place. He'd never known dogs and cats to get along.

But it was more than that. A cage of sorts was fastened on the back of the wagon, full of chickens. Two cows were also tied to the back of the wagon. Clearly these people were the thrifty sort and intended to supply the businesses in Blessings with much-needed milk and eggs. But they would soon find that the landscape was ill-suited to such endeavors, the winters too cold, too harsh. But he had to admire their strength and spirit for trying. Clarissa had often commented what she wouldn't give for some fresh eggs. He would do well to befriend these people. Though he knew the price for eggs would be dear, perhaps such luxury would bring a smile to his sister's face once more.

One of the ladies was holding a chicken like it was a baby. Clearly the family was most unusual indeed. But weren't they all? Everyone thought he was crazy for bringing his children here. A wise man would have left them back in San Francisco with Clarissa. But they were his only tie to Lily. More than that, he genuinely loved his children, and enjoyed their company. They told such stories, and he found that he enjoyed their funny games. It didn't seem like many fathers took such delight in their family, or at least it seemed like others thought him a fool for doing so. But how could he think himself a fool, when he knew life was so fleeting, and so precious?

Atherton had helped him and his family get their start here, hiring him to work on his house, then recommending his work to others. It seemed only right that he allow the man to bless someone else. The town was, after all, named Blessings.

"It'll be good to have more neighbors," he said pleasantly, then looked over his children. "I hope they haven't been giving you any trouble."

One of the women, the one not holding the chicken, with dark hair, bright eyes, and a pleasant look about her stepped forward. "Not at all. They're delightful. I love children. You and your wife must be very proud."

He tried not to sigh at her assumption. Everyone assumed. And he didn't mind it so much, because it numbed him to his loss. Being reminded so many times that he was completely alone made him used to the fact. Though of course, he wasn't completely alone. He had his sister and the children.

But sometimes, he thought about how it would be nice to have a warm body next to him in the bed, someone he could turn to, and speak of his dreams, hopes, wishes, and fears. He was doing everything he could to make a life for his family. And if Blessings continued growing the way Atherton had told him he'd hoped it would, this would be a perfect place to make that life.

What were the hopes and dreams of this family?

Atherton was right that the small cabin and large shed that someone had once hoped to turn into a livery was a temporary stop for such people. It was too small of a lot to maintain these animals for too long, but it would be perfect for him once he had the funds to purchase it. He was looking forward to turning the large shed into a workshop so he could begin making the fine furniture pieces he enjoyed spending his time on. He supposed it didn't matter much now, considering his carpentry business was keeping him too busy to take on pet projects.

Some of the jobs, like framing houses, were tedious and dull. But the owner of the new hotel was looking for someone to do custom mantel pieces and trim in the rooms to give it a more sophisticated look. He was looking forward to the challenge.

"I'm Tom Davidson," the young man said, stepping forward. "And these are my sisters Louisa and Josephine."

Tom looked barely older than a boy, but the full beard told him that the poor fellow was a man. And by the looks of things, one just trying to provide for his family. Though his and Clarissa's parents hadn't died until after he'd married, he still knew what it felt like to want to take care of one's sister. It was nice to know he already had something in common with his new neighbor.

"Jonah Hastings. It's a pleasure to meet you. These are my children, Nathaniel and Callie, and my sister, Clarissa, lives with us as well."

He turned to Louisa and smiled. "My wife passed away over a year ago, but I'm sure she would be very proud of the children. Clarissa does a wonderful job caring for them. I'm surprised you haven't met her yet."

He turned and looked toward the house, wondering why she hadn't yet come out. Surely she would be curious about where the children had gotten off to and what they were doing. At the very least, she would have seen that there were strangers and wanted to investigate.

He'd have liked to have gone in to check on her, but it would be rude to leave their guests. Instead, he turned to them. "Can we invite you in for some refreshment? It won't take long to put on some coffee for the men and tea for the ladies."

The Davidson family looked at each other, then back at him. "We thank you for your kind invitation," Tom said. "But as we only have just a few more hours left of daylight, we need to make this place habitable, so we have a place to sleep for the evening. And we'll have to tend to our animals as well. I hope you don't think us too rude. We would be happy to take you up on your offer as well as have you over sometime in the future."

Surely they didn't intend to stay in the cabin tonight. Jonah looked over at the ramshackle building. He'd taken down the more dangerous loose boards, as he knew the children sometimes played there. But it wasn't a place he would recommend anyone spend the night, let alone a young man and two young ladies. One of their cows let out a long bellow, reminding him that, with their animals, they likely didn't have many other options. They could always sleep in the wagon, but they'd probably already done that a number of nights already.

As he gave the property a quick look, he realized that would most likely be the first priority. Much of the fencing was down and securing the barn area would be important for the safety of the animals and for keeping them from getting loose. The family would likely have to sleep in the wagon another night.

He should be getting back to work. He'd only come home for lunch because his current job was only a block away, so it was more convenient to come home to eat, spend a little time with his family, then get back to work.

But helping this family was the right thing to do. The neighborly thing to do. He was ahead of schedule on his other job, so missing a half-day's work wouldn't put anyone out.

"I understand completely," Jonah said. "In fact, I was just thinking that I should give you a hand. Atherton is right in that I would eventually like to purchase this property. It seems only right that I assist with the improvements."

Atherton studied him, then looked over the family. Then back at him. He'd heard that the old man prided himself in matchmaking. Was he already making plans? Both girls were pretty enough, but Josephine, still clutching her chicken, seemed a bit too eccentric for his tastes. And while there was something definitely pleasant about Louisa, he was a man with a family, responsibilities. Romance was not on his list.

"I wouldn't want to impose," Tom said, but there was hesitation on his face, like he was unsure about what he was doing, and needed the help, but didn't want to say so.

Jonah had seen a lot of men like Tom here. Men whose pride prevented them from accepting help and then ended up in trouble because of it. The men who'd tried to turn this place into a livery, for example. Because the building had been so substandard, some of it had caved in during the first heavy snow. It was a danger to them all. And one young man, with only the assistance of two young ladies who had probably never done a hard day's worth of work in their lives, were ill-prepared for the necessary repairs.

"It's no trouble. I'm a carpenter. And it will be of great assistance to me if you allow me to help you. Then, when people compliment you on getting this place habitable so quickly, you can give them my name, and it will help me gain more business. A winning proposition for us all."

He didn't need the business, in fact, he turned many customers away, and had a long waiting list for his services. It wasn't just that a booming town such as this needed carpenters, but everyone said he did fine work. Some might think it was prideful of him to say so, but the good Lord had given him a talent, and it seemed wrong to acknowledge people's compliments without thanking God for giving him such ability. The gifts he had were from God, and he was grateful God had given him the ability to provide so well for his family.

Once again, the Davidson siblings looked at each other in such a way that he thought they must have some sort of secret signal or code. He envied that closeness. He'd always wanted to have a similar closeness to his sister. They'd had it as children, but, when he married, his sister and his late wife did not get along well, and Clarissa had to distance herself from him. He'd hoped that with Clarissa caring for his children, they would regain some of that closeness. But it often felt like they didn't really know each other anymore.

"We would be grateful for your assistance," Tom said. "My sisters and I, while we have done a great deal of work on our father's farm, do not know the finer points of carpentry. I'm sure you will be able to give us tips on how best to repair our home so that we have a safe and comfortable place to live. I understand the winters are cold here, and we will need to be sure we are well protected."

It was good to see that he was a man of sense. One of the things Jonah had learned since coming to Blessings was that men of sense were few and far between when there was gold nearby. The lore of riches clouded a man's judgment and blinded him to practicalities. So many had come and gone, but already he found himself liking this family, and hoped they would stay.

As he and Tom walked the property, and he made suggestions to Tom, he noticed that Tom's sisters followed him closely. It seemed that they were just as interested in what they needed to do as he was, and when Tom went to lift one of the fallen fence posts, Louisa was quick to jump in to help. Josephine hung back, but that was probably because she still held the chicken. Every once in a while she would give it a little pet, then say something softly to it as if it understood.

Louisa must've caught him staring, because after they moved the post, she turned to him. "I know it looks odd, but Josephine has a way with animals. Esmeralda is her favorite bird, but the other chickens pick on her. So she can't keep her in the cage with them. And she can't let her loose, because she startles easily, and when she gets startled, she hides in strange places, and it takes forever to find her. I know it sounds silly, but with our father's death, we lost everything, Josephine the most of all. We had to sell or give away almost all our other animals. So I'll do everything in my power to help her keep as many of what we have remaining as possible."

Such compassion was a rare thing in this world, especially in a town like this, where people were here for their own gain. True, Atherton was doing his best to change that attitude, and to create a real community. Jonah wanted to be part of that community, and it started here, with this family.

CHAPTER 2

*T*hanks to Jonah's help, they'd gotten settled in their home rather quickly. Mr. Winslet, rather, Atherton, as he'd asked them to call him, had referred a number of miners to them for laundry. It was a respectable job, and though Louisa's hands were raw and aching most days, it did provide a good source of income. Tom had easily found work in the mines, and though people used to tease her for being large for a woman, the people in the mines commented on her being small for a man. Her smallness though, provided useful, and Tom was often scurrying about in the tight places other men couldn't reach.

They'd learned during their travels that asking questions about their father would get them nowhere, so here in Blessing, they tried a different tactic. The ladies were getting to know the miners who dropped off the laundry. The men were all too eager to tell them about themselves, their lives, and all sorts of personal information they would have never told someone investigating a murder. Of course, these men were hoping that their answers would please Louisa and Josephine, and they would allow them to court them.

None of these miners were the sort of men to interest Louisa or Josephine, though. Louisa hoping for someone a little more cultured, someone she could discuss her favorite books with, and who would understand her desire to become a teacher. Since most schools required that teachers remain unmarried, it seemed unfair to even look for a man. Josephine still longed to return to a life on a farm or on a ranch. Neither would become a miner's bride.

As Louisa hung yet another load of laundry out to dry, she glanced over at Jonah's house. He hadn't given any indication of being interested in her, and it would be improper for her to pursue him. But she'd be lying if she said she didn't like him. Strange, considering she hardly saw him. They'd been in Blessings nearly a month now, and she'd barely spoken to him. His children said he worked a lot.

Little Callie was a chatterbox, constantly coming over to tell her stories. As for Jonah's sister, Clarissa, other than the time she'd had the family over for dinner, Louisa hadn't seen her. The children said their aunt slept a lot.

As if the thought had conjured them, Callie and Nathaniel bounded over. "Miss Louisa. Will you play a game with us?"

The children were constantly asking her this question. Everywhere she went, children seemed to flock to her. It was one of the reasons she knew she was destined to become a schoolteacher.

She liked children and children liked her. It was a shame they didn't have a schoolhouse here in Blessings. Louisa had asked Atherton about one, and he'd told her with a sigh, "Maybe someday."

Perhaps, once the family's situation was a little more stable, she would approach Atherton and ask him if he might consider allowing her to teach a few classes. As she looked at the clearing between her house and Jonah's house, she could see a place for little benches where children could sit for lessons.

"Miss Louisa." Callie's voice had taken a plaintive note. Little Nathaniel looked up at her with the kind of wide eyes the dogs gave her in the evenings when they were having their supper.

Which is when she had an idea.

"Have you ever been to school?"

Nathaniel was a bit on the young side for school, but Louisa was of an age that she should have gone.

Both children shook their heads.

"All right then. I have work to do, and I've decided that you will have to earn the opportunity to play games."

She hung the last shirt on the line, then gestured to the house. "Come. Let's see what kind of books I have."

Louisa let the children inside, where they'd turned the drab, dilapidated cabin into a home. Jonah had promised them that when he had some spare time, he would add on a bedroom so the ladies wouldn't have to sleep in the loft, separated by a curtain from their brother. Poor Jonah seemed very concerned with propriety. And it wasn't that they weren't, but needs being what they were, and the conditions of the mining camp, it simply wasn't practical.

In hopes of becoming a schoolteacher, Louisa had collected a number of books suitable for various ages. She'd also acquired other school supplies, thinking that if she ever had a student in need, she would be able to help him or her. Perhaps it wasn't a traditional school house, but good could be done here. She brought out the slates, tucked inside her trunk, and led the children back outside, setting the children down on a nearby log. Then she wrote each child's name.

"We're going to start by learning to write your names. Do you see what I've written here?"

Dark, eager heads nodded.

"Now I want you to copy what I've done."

"I know how to write my name," Callie said. "My mother taught me."

They'd never spoken of their mother, but Louisa understood that she'd been gone quite some time. Still, it was encouraging that the children at least had a basic foundation from which to build upon.

"That's excellent news. Why don't you write your name for me, then perhaps you can write a few other things, just to demonstrate what you know."

Callie nodded, then looked over at her brother. "I've tried teaching him his letters, but he isn't very good yet."

Louisa smiled at them. "Then we shall both teach him. Just do your best, so I can see where we need to do more work."

Once the children murmured their agreement, Louisa went back to work on the laundry. Her brief interlude with the children had given the shirts she was washing time to soak, something they had desperately needed. So many of the miners' clothing they took in were so dirty by the time they got the chance to wash them, they could have almost walked off on their own. As she scrubbed the shirts, the children returned to her side.

"We finished," Callie said. "Now what?"

She hadn't had time to think of their next lesson, beyond the fact that she wanted to evaluate where they were. And she still had to finish this tub of laundry.

"Why don't we sing some songs?"

She began to sing the opening bars of the alphabet song, pleased to note that the children joined in enthusiastically, and seemed to know all the words. At least they knew their letters.

She sang other songs, ones she had learned from her mother, and others she'd learned in school. She liked singing while she worked, though it had been a while since she'd thought of these songs. Still, it was good, combining her work with songs that could teach the children. At least it was keeping them occupied.

She glanced over at their house.

It was a shame Clarissa hadn't yet looked out to see them. Louisa hated to think ill of anyone, but it bothered her that Jonah said Clarissa was in charge of their care while he worked, and yet Louisa never saw her. The children ran practically wild, and Clarissa never seemed to notice.

There were so many ways a child could be put in danger, especially in a rough town like this. And, with the river just yards behind them, the children could easily fall in and drown.

Perhaps she was being too judgmental. But, there was the children's safety to think of. Did Jonah know that the children often ran about on their own, with Clarissa nowhere to be seen?

Was it her place to say something?

Though she knew Jonah cared about his children, it frustrated her that he had so little care for their safety. As if to prove her point, gunshots rang out in the distance. Judging from the direction of the sound, it had likely come from the saloon, which didn't come as a surprise in this tiny town. Though Atherton had done a wonderful job in hiring Sheriff Pete Jones to keep peace and order, the mining lifestyle invited an unsavory element to any mining community. Saloons and houses of ill repute, while not as numerous in Blessings, attracted unsavory sorts.

It was one of the reasons they'd felt good about Tom's disguise. Three women traveling alone were easy targets for those people. But two women, under the protection of a man, were less likely to be accosted. As she looked over at the children, she couldn't help wondering about the unsavory people who might wish to do them harm. She'd read that children as young as Nathaniel and Callie were often sent to work in the mines as well as other unsafe places because their small bodies could get where men couldn't. It was dangerous work, and some children did not enter it willingly. Had Jonah considered these things when allowing his children to run wild?

As if to prove her point, the children began climbing a tree in their backyard. Or at least trying to. Callie had boosted her brother up on her shoulders and Nathaniel was reaching for one of the upper branches. Louisa took a step toward them just as Nathaniel tumbled off Callie's shoulders. She ran to them. "Nathaniel! Are you all right?"

The little boy started to cry. "My head hurts."

She quickly felt the spot where he indicated. No blood. But that didn't mean a lump wouldn't form.

"Let's get you a cool cloth, and you can lie down." She picked the little boy up and carried him to his house. She knocked on the door, but there was no answer.

Callie tugged at her skirts. "Auntie doesn't like to be disturbed. She'll be angry if we wake her."

She stared at the little girl. "But your brother's hurt. Surely she should care about that."

Callie looked frightened. "I wouldn't bother her."

"What about your father?"

Callie shook her head furiously. "We mustn't bother him. He gets very angry when we disturb his work."

She supposed she could understand that. After all, with his kind of work, it was no place for a child. But what kept Clarissa so occupied that she wouldn't want to care for her injured nephew?

Louisa rapped on the door again.

Callie hid behind her skirts. "I don't want to be in trouble."

She heard a shuffling, then the door flew open. Clarissa was still in her dressing gown. "What have they gotten into now?"

Louisa still held the whimpering little boy to her chest. "The children were climbing a tree, and Nathaniel took a fall. I don't believe he's injured too seriously, but it would be best to watch him to be sure. I believe he will have a nasty bump on his head later. A cool cloth should help keep it from becoming too serious."

Clarissa yawned. "Do you think I should call Dr. Edwards?"

"I don't believe so, as he didn't lose consciousness. But you know him best, so you should watch him and see if he acts unusually or has other symptoms that warrant a doctor."

Clarissa yawned again. Had Louisa just gotten the woman out of bed? It was nearly noon. Surely the other woman wasn't such a slugabed. Did she really value her sleep over the safety of her niece and nephew?

"I told you two to behave yourselves," Clarissa said. "Why can't you listen?"

She held out her arms for Nathaniel. "I'll take him. I'm sure he'll be fine. But I thank you for your concern."

Clarissa ushered Callie in, then closed the door firmly behind her. Louisa hated leaving Callie, when she had that terrified look on her face. She'd only been thinking of Nathaniel's safety, but she wondered if she'd made the right decision.

She was still fretting about the children when she arrived home. Josephine was elbow deep in a basin of laundry.

"Can you run to the mercantile to see if the extra buttons we ordered are in? My supply is getting woefully low, and Bill's shirts are in need of repair. I don't know how that man loses so many buttons, but he always pays a great deal extra to have me put more on."

"Of course. I'm happy to do it."

She didn't say so to her sister, but it would give her a chance to go by where Jonah was working, and perhaps she could have a word with him. It seemed wrong to interfere, but she was also concerned for the little boy's safety.

As she walked toward Main Street, and down to where Jonah was working on the hotel, she saw him entering the saloon with a group of gentlemen.

The saloon?

She'd thought him a better man than that, and it was sad to see that instead of working hard the way he said he did, he was taking in entertainments.

His poor children.

Especially when Nathaniel was injured.

It simply wouldn't do.

Louisa stormed across the street and entered the saloon. She'd never been inside such a place before, and no proper lady would ever be seen setting foot there. But this was an emergency. For such a serious matter, propriety would have to wait.

As she entered the saloon, the place grew silent. Everyone in the room turned to look at her. Including Jonah.

She walked right up to him. "I cannot believe you are in such a place. Your children have been running wild again. Today, they were climbing a tree, and Nathaniel fell and hit his head. I brought them to your house, and your sister had clearly just woken up. She answered the door in her dressing gown. Though I don't believe Nathaniel's injuries are serious, I do hope you will look after him. It is a shame the way your children are neglected."

Before he could answer, she turned and marched out the door. It wasn't until she found herself outside and, on the street, staring at Atherton Winslet, that she realized how foolish she must've looked.

"Atherton. I..."

What could she say? She was a lady, walking out of the saloon. After all her brother had done to emphasize their respectability, she'd just gone and completely ruined her reputation. But it was for a worthy cause.

She squared her shoulders as she stared at him. "I do apologize for my unseemly behavior, however I felt it important to let Jonah know that not only were his children running wild again, but his son was just injured falling from a tree. I do not like what goes on at that house. Those children need guidance. And I find it scandalous that instead of providing said guidance to his children, Jonah is spending time in the saloon."

As she turned and walked away, she thought she heard Atherton chuckle. Chuckle! Apparently, she was the only person in town concerned with the safety of others.

No wonder they didn't have a school.

CHAPTER 3

*W*hat had just happened? Jonah stared after the saloon door at the swishing skirts of the angry woman who'd just left.

Nathaniel was hurt?

Surely Clarissa could handle it. It was her job, after all.

But then, he had to wonder. If Nathaniel was injured badly enough that Louisa had felt it necessary to take it upon herself to chastise him, perhaps it was something more serious. He looked over at Shen Wu. He'd invited him to the saloon, along with George Willis, the owner of the blacksmith shop, to discuss plans for repairs to the shop.

He hated to leave. They'd struggled for weeks, trying to find a time where they could all sit down together, mostly because George was often too drunk to put a coherent sentence together. Shen was his assistant, and though Jonah would mostly be working with him, the boss still needed to approve the plans.

"I hate to do this, but it appears my son is injured, and I need to check on him."

Shen nodded. "It seems to be serious indeed. Your wife looked quite angry."

"She's not my wife. Just a neighbor." Even though he'd spoken accurately, something about his words rang false. He'd barely spoken to Louisa, yet there was something about her, something that made him wonder

Ridiculous. He shouldn't think of such things, not about Louisa, and not when his son needed him.

When Jonah arrived home, Clarissa was fixing lunch for the children. The chaotic scene he'd expected based on Louisa's description was nowhere to be found. He didn't think Louisa had been lying, but perhaps she'd over exaggerated, or at the very least, overreacted.

"I understand Nathaniel was injured," he said, looking at his son. Nathaniel was sitting at the table, patiently waiting for whatever Clarissa was going to be serving. When his son turned, he could see the bruise on the little boy's head.

"I fell from the tree," Nathaniel said. "Callie didn't catch me."

"You weren't supposed to fall." Callie looked indignant, like it was a greater travesty that her brother was blaming her than his injury itself.

"What were you even doing, climbing the tree? It's not safe. I've told you that several times now."

He looked over at Clarissa. "And what were you thinking, letting them do it?"

Clarissa let out a long sigh. "One does not let the children do anything. They have minds of their own, and they don't listen."

That was Clarissa's most common answer. Whenever he got on her about them running wild, she always had the same excuse: that they didn't listen. But they listened just fine for him. It seemed like no matter how many times he told the children to listen to Clarissa, she continued claiming they didn't.

He turned his attention back to the children. "What did your Aunt Clarissa say to you?"

Callie looked defiant, squaring her shoulders, and straightening. "She didn't tell us anything. She was in bed. We didn't even have any breakfast. I just wanted Nathaniel to climb the tree to see if he could see where you're working, that's all."

Clarissa glared at them. "You know very well that if I'm asleep, you are not to go outside. And as for your breakfast, there were biscuits on the counter for you."

"But no jam," Nathaniel muttered.

Clarissa stood. "If you two hadn't sneaked it and eaten it all the other day, we would still have some."

"I know there's more," Callie said. "You're just being selfish."

"We only have so much jam to last. If I brought out more every time the two of you snuck the jam and ate it all, we'd have none left."

The argument was a familiar one, and it was frustrating how the children and Clarissa bickered. It was almost as if Clarissa was one of the children herself. On one hand, Clarissa was right. The children shouldn't be sneaking jam, and rationing it was a good idea. But she didn't need to keep arguing with them about it.

"You children know you need to respect your aunt. If you've been taking jam without her permission, then it serves you right to not have any. We're fortunate to even have biscuits. You should be grateful that she takes such good care of you."

The children looked at each other in a funny way but didn't say anything. He liked that they were close, but so many times, it seemed like they were conspiring against him.

And there was still the matter of sneaking out of the house.

"And you two should know better than to sneak out of the house without your aunt's permission. It's not safe for you to be running wild through the streets."

"We weren't running through the streets," Callie said. "We were in the yard. No one ever said we can't be in the yard."

Technically, she was right. In all his warnings for them against running wild in the streets, Jonah always told them to stay in the yard.

"But Clarissa told you to stay inside, isn't that right?"

Callie smiled. "Aunt Clarissa didn't say anything. She was asleep."

He looked over at Clarissa. "Is this true?"

"Yes, but they know to stay inside while I'm asleep. She's just doing what she always does, trying to find a loophole to stay out of trouble."

Jonah let out a long sigh. Clarissa was right. However, Callie was also technically right. So it was time to close the loophole.

"Well, then. It seems we need to make the rules a little clearer for Callie and Nathaniel. You may not leave the house when your aunt is asleep. You will have to find some other way of entertaining yourselves until she wakes up. Is that clear?"

Two dark heads nodded. "Yes Papa," they said in unison.

Throughout the conversation, he's been watching Nathaniel, to see if he'd suffered any ill effects from falling and hitting his head. He could see none. The boy appeared in full control of his faculties. However, what if he was wrong? Nathaniel might be a handful, but he couldn't imagine his life without the dear little boy.

"How are you feeling, Nathaniel? Does your head bother you much?"

"It's just a bump," Clarissa said. "Really, Jonah, you have to stop coddling them. Think of all the bruises and scrapes you got as a child. Why, I remember the time you broke your arm, trying to get the cherries from the very top of the cherry tree. Now who does that sound like?"

He smiled at the memory. In some ways Nathaniel and Callie reminded him a lot of him and Clarissa as children. Clarissa egging him on to do something silly, like getting the cherries that no one else could reach, even though they'd been warned not to climb the tree.

But these were not stories to be told in front of the children. Now they were going to think that their mischief was all right.

"I just want to be sure he's not more badly injured. I know some children like to pretend to be sick to get out of things, but I've noticed that these two, much like we did when we were younger, pretend not to be sick or injured because they don't want anything interfering with their activities."

He ruffled his son's hair, smiling down at him. "You will tell us if your head continues to bother you, won't you? I think, to be on the safe side, you and your sister should spend the rest the day indoors, with your aunt, and you can do a quiet activity."

"But we had the game we were playing." Callie jumped up out of her seat. "And I'm not the one who was injured. I shouldn't be punished for his injury."

"Yes, but you did have a role in it. As the eldest, you shouldn't have encouraged your brother to climb the tree. You have just as much of a part in it as he did."

As he looked around the kitchen, he could see that the place was in general need of tidying up. Clarissa wasn't a good housekeeper on the best of days, but lately, her skills seemed to have been slipping, a fact he hadn't mentioned to her, because he didn't want her to think he was ungrateful for her help.

He turned his attention back to the children. "In fact, it looks like your aunt could use some help with the chores around the house. Obviously, we'll want Nathaniel to only do the very simple tasks, so that he doesn't pain his head too much. But, Callie, I believe you can help her with some of her other more difficult things. I'm sure it will help the work go faster, and then perhaps, when I get home this evening, we can all sing some songs. I'll even get out my fiddle."

A mixture of emotions crossed the children's faces and made him smile. They did hate to work, but they also loved when Jonah got out his fiddle. When Lily was alive, they did it every night. But since her death, the joy he found in music was no longer there. Growing up, his family had always had something musical going on. He and Clarissa had always been singing, playing instruments, or even just humming a tune. But since Lily's death, it was like the music had left him. Even Clarissa seemed to feel the loss, because he hadn't heard her sing since she'd come to live with them.

But at his suggestion, Clarissa shook her head. "I don't know that they deserve to have such a fun evening after all the trouble they've gotten into today."

Of all things he hated the most about losing the music, it was Clarissa's loss. She'd always had a beautiful voice, and were it a respectable profession, he could easily see her gracing the stages around the world, providing delightful entertainment to thousands. And even though their parents were now gone, she could still hear his mother saying that such activities were shameful for women.

"But they'll work hard for you this afternoon," Jonah said. "I'm confident of it."

The resigned expression on Clarissa's face made him wish he hadn't made the suggestion. He did miss her singing. But perhaps, if she really wasn't up for it later, he would at least play his fiddle, sing with the children, and try to remember the happier times.

He glanced out the window, and could see Louisa by the river, scrubbing laundry. It was kind of her to be so concerned about his children, but having come home and seen for himself, he had to say that he thought she'd overreacted. Especially since his leaving had cost him a meeting he'd been so desperately trying to get.

Hopefully he could meet with Shen and George again soon. And even though they'd already indicated to him that they'd like him to do the job, hopefully his running out like that didn't make them think he was unreliable and unable to do the work.

Callie tugged at his hand. "I'm sorry Papa. We didn't mean to cause so much trouble. But now that you're home, would you play a game with us?"

He shook his head. "I'd like to, but I have a lot of work to get done. I only came because Louisa had told me there was an emergency, and I wanted to be sure Nathaniel was safe."

Clarissa groaned. "That Louisa. A busybody if I ever knew one. Oh, she acts all neighborly and concerned. But I think she's like one of those busybodies from back home, not content with minding her own business, but having to get herself mixed up in everyone else's. I don't know why she just can't leave well enough alone."

Though Clarissa's words were harsh, Nathaniel had to admit that while he thought Louisa's interference a bit much, he also believed her heart was in the right place. She seemed like a good person, and when he saw her interacting with his children, she seemed genuinely compassionate and caring. In fact, when he'd worked on the Davidson house, she often kept the children out of the way. He liked that she treated them as human beings, and not annoyances.

He gave Clarissa a smile. "I don't believe she means any harm. She seems to genuinely care about the children, and I'm sure she was only worried about their safety."

Clarissa let out a long sigh. "You're sweet on her, aren't you? It's just like a man, to be so easily influenced by a pretty face. I think that she only uses the children as an excuse to get close to you."

Had his sister grown daft all of a sudden?

"That's the most ridiculous thing you've ever said. She might be pretty enough to look at, but you and I both know that handsome is as handsome does. I don't know Louisa well enough to have formed much of an opinion on her character, and I don't intend to do so. Lily was the love of my life, and I have no desire to pursue anyone else. I'm content with what I have, so don't read anything into my actions that aren't there. As for Louisa, she's never given me any indication of anything but neighborly feelings."

It was tempting to add that when Atherton had made a comment about him finding love with the Davidson sisters, Louisa had rolled her eyes and walked away. She was just as uninterested in romance as he was. But to say so to Clarissa would only be adding fuel to the fire. She would see his denials as protesting too much, but in his case, his protests were genuine.

Clarissa just shook her head. "I've got eyes, the same as anyone else. And I see the way you look at her."

Considering he hardly ever saw her, that was a strange accusation. And once again, completely unfounded.

Obviously, Clarissa was trying to take attention off the fact that the children had escaped her watchful eye once more. But that was a different conversation for a different time.

He looked at his pocket watch. "I'm afraid I really do have to go now. I was going to have lunch with the gentlemen at the saloon, and now my lunch time is past. Please children, do be good for your aunt so my work isn't interrupted again."

Clarissa gave him a sympathetic glance. "Take this biscuit and some ham. At least it will be something to fill your stomach until supper. I was going to prepare a venison stew."

Not his favorite, but so far outside civilization, there weren't many other food choices. They were lucky to have venison, as many didn't have even that much. In fact, they were fortunate that he had so much work. He'd remembered enough lean years that he knew this was a blessing indeed. He gratefully accepted the lunch Clarissa prepared for him and said a silent prayer of thanks to God for protecting his family and watching out for them.

Maybe the life he dreamed of building with Lily was impossible, but at least he had his children and his work. The life he imagined was not to be, but God had a different plan for him, and he had to continue trusting in God's goodness and believe that someday, he would understand God's plan for all of it.

As he stepped out onto the porch, he caught Louisa's eye. He was too angry with her to speak to her yet. She had no idea what she'd interrupted, and for such a minor thing. It was nice that she cared enough about his son to think it serious enough to get him, but Clarissa did have things in hand. However, as he walked toward the street, she came to him.

"Is Nathaniel going to be all right? I didn't see the doctor, so I'm hoping he is well."

The genuine concern on her face made Nathaniel let out a long sigh. How could he fault a woman for caring about his son?

"He appears quite well. Clarissa has everything nicely in hand, and he is now enjoying his lunch. Though I appreciate your concern for my children, I would also appreciate if, in

47

the future, you do not send for me unless Clarissa has asked you to. You interrupted a very important business meeting, and I do not believe it was necessary."

Anger flashed in her eyes.

"A business meeting. Is that what you call it? Fine. I was only acting out of concern for your son's well-being, but I can see you have more important things on your mind."

She turned on her heel and stomped off, back to her laundry. He'd have liked to have stopped her, to tell her how wrong she was, that his children were his first priority, but he could sense Clarissa watching from the windows. He didn't need to add fuel to the fire of her thinking there was anything between him and Louisa.

Besides, what did he care what Louisa Davidson thought of him? She was just a meddling neighbor. She might care about his children, and he couldn't fault her for that. But she had no business butting into his.

Still, as he continued down the street to his job site, he couldn't help thinking of all the things he would say in his defense. Couldn't help wanting her to see him in a better light.

But that wasn't because he had any feelings for her. It couldn't be.

CHAPTER 4

*O*f all the nerve. Louisa stomped back to where she'd been doing laundry. Josephine was sitting under the tree, holding one of her chickens.

"Those were some sparks," Josephine said. "What's going on?"

"I told you how little Nathaniel had been injured earlier today. Well, I happened upon Jonah when I was in town, and he was at the saloon. Can you believe it? The saloon. In the middle of the day. So of course, I had to make sure he knew about Nathaniel's injury. What kind of father would rather be in the saloon instead of watching his children?"

Josephine set the chicken down and stood, brushing off her skirts. "It sounds like you've come to a lot of conclusions. Did you discuss this with him?"

"Why should I? It seems to me the situation was quite obvious. He was walking to the saloon, and his son was at home hurt. Moreover, I did tell you that when I brought the children home to let them know of Nathaniel's injury, Clarissa had obviously still been in bed. Who was watching his children?"

Josephine sighed. "You don't know the full of the situation. You shouldn't judge them. Not just because the Bible tells us that, but because we have faced a great deal of judgment in our time, and we know how horrible it is. Perhaps Clarissa wasn't feeling well. Perhaps Jonah's visit to the saloon was to meet with people who chose that as a meeting location. It isn't as though we have a great deal of fine dining establishments or other suitable places for business meetings. You know how men are. Even father, who refused to drink, often met with people in saloons for business reasons. It isn't good of you to think so ill of our neighbors. We hardly know them, and it won't do for us to make enemies of them. Particularly when Jonah has been so helpful."

Louisa hated that her sister was correct. "Perhaps I did overreact. I'm sometimes blinded to reason when it comes to the safety and security of children."

Another chicken ambled toward Josephine, and Josephine bent to pick it up. "I do know what you mean. I feel the same way about animals. I know people don't understand it, and I content myself with that, because my animal friends have no one but me to speak for them."

She gave the chicken a little pat, then let it run free. "You would not believe how much money one of the Chinamen offered me for a chicken. He kept mumbling something incomprehensible about the chicken's feet. Why on earth would I let him have my chicken's feet? I can't even imagine."

Louisa didn't have the heart to tell her sister that there were actually many recipes that she'd seen in a magazine featuring chicken feet. Apparently, they were quite useful, but it was something the family had not learned for themselves. Because of Josephine's love for the animals, they didn't eat much meat. Instead they ate lots of vegetables and eggs. Occasionally they got away with serving meat that wasn't personally known to Josephine.

But they never ate chicken.

She'd read about people who considered cows as so sacred that they couldn't be eaten, as part of the religious belief they held. Louisa often wondered if Josephine's love of chickens and refusal to eat them was part of her beliefs in God.

In a way, it did make sense. After all, she'd read a book about St. Francis of Assisi, and how he loved the animals. He ate no meat, and she had to think that were it not for her family forcing her to do so, Josephine would follow the same path.

"I have the last of the laundry drying," Josephine said. "The work went more quickly today, and I'm eager for the miners to come and get their clothing. One of them, Miguel Hernandez, commented to me about Zeus. He told me that he grew up on a ranch, and he also had a dog similar to Zeus. He couldn't stop talking about how much he loved being on his old ranch, but it had been taken from him. I couldn't help feeling a certain sympathy for him, as his family's plight is so similar to ours. Small ranchers and farmers can't compete with the bigger operations moving in, then buying up the land when it's foreclosed upon."

Once again, Josephine had found someone who loved animals.

"What does that have to do with our investigation?" Louisa asked.

Josephine shrugged. "If he was a rancher, perhaps he knows people who might have been robbed and killed like father was. You heard what that sheriff said. Things like that happen all the time, and they can't possibly devote the kind of resources to looking into it. Perhaps, if I can get Miguel to talk about his family, his former community, and how things might have been, he might say something about other people who are robbed and murdered, and that might give us clues about our father's death."

Because of Josephine's devotion to the animals, many people considered her a simpleton. They mistook her quietness for lack of education, and, because she was a woman, no one suspected that she, like her sisters, had been classically educated. No one would suspect her of digging deeper into their father's death.

There were a lot of things no one would suspect the Davidson sisters of. Tom seemed to be fitting in well with the other men, even so far as being invited out to the saloon. And when he did not participate in the antics of liquor and women, many of the others just assumed that he was a religious man.

Which, surprisingly, was not uncommon in this town. Though many of the men led sinful lives while professing faith in Christ, there were many others, like the man Tom pretended to be, who seemed to have a deep abiding love of the Lord that extended to all their actions.

One more reason why Josephine had been correct in chastising her. To live in such a godless town, one needed to rise above and show the love of Christ. It did no one any good to fight evil with evil, a fact she'd known all her life, but for some reason, where their neighbors were concerned, she'd been doing a very poor job indeed.

"You're staring at their house like you want to kill them," Josephine said. "You've got to let this go. I know you're worried about the children, but don't let your anger take over."

"That's exactly what I was thinking," Louisa said, turning back to her sister. "I was terribly wrong in jumping to conclusions, then taking Jonah to task for it. We were raised better than that, and I was just thinking that if we are to be in the midst of such an ungodly place, we should hold firm to our beliefs, and live them out in such a way as to be shining example to others."

Josephine nodded. "It's difficult not to live in condemnation of others and choose to love them instead. But that is what the Lord asks of us, even when it's difficult."

Josephine's words confirmed what Louisa already knew. She owed Jonah an apology. Clarissa too, even though she especially hated the idea. Clarissa just seemed to have a haughtiness about her, like she was above everyone else. And she certainly acted like Louisa or anyone else had no right questioning her. But then again, Louisa didn't have the right.

So perhaps Clarissa was justified in her hostility toward her. Perhaps the negative attitude Louisa received from Clarissa was in response to Louisa's unkindness to her. Not that Louisa had been deliberately unkind. But she also hadn't been very welcoming either. She certainly hadn't been trying to be very understanding of the other woman. She knew nothing about her, and she hadn't tried. But she would rectify that fact.

Louisa gathered the rest of her washing things and followed Josephine back into the house.

"I know how dear our eggs are. But I was wondering if we could perhaps spare a few to bring over to the neighbors. They're dear to everyone here, and perhaps I could give them some eggs as a gift along with my apology as a way to ease our relation."

Josephine nodded slowly. "I was hoping that Henrietta would go broody again and hatch a few more, because I do so dearly love baby chicks. But they've only just started laying again, after the trauma of being forced from their home and into a new environment. Tom has been telling me that I'm being stingy with our eggs, and that it would be a nice show of goodwill to our neighbors and friends if we were to share them. I've been thinking that she was being too harsh and judgmental with me, but after the dressing down I just gave you, I'm starting to think that perhaps Tom was right."

Josephine gave a halfhearted smile as she reached for the basket containing their eggs. "I suppose we all have a great deal of growing and learning to do. But that is why I'm so thankful that God loves us anyway. He knows our faults, and he's chosen to love us, even though we make so many mistakes. Let's put a basket together. We'll give them some eggs, but I've also been wanting to do some baking. I don't wish to give eggs to all our friends and neighbors, because we really don't have enough. Why don't you and I spend the rest of the day doing some baking? I'm sure it will be a treat to everyone who's helped us to receive some baked goods."

Josephine's acquiescence warmed her heart. She was right in that they were all having to learn and do difficult things. Tom especially. She'd caught the longing look on her sister's face when Louisa and Josephine helped each other with their hair. It used to be something the three of them did together, taking turns with different hairstyles, discussing the latest fashions. There was no money to be spent on clothing, and it didn't seem fair for Louisa and Josephine to get new dresses anyway, not with Tom being unable to enjoy them. Of all the sisters, it was Tom who enjoyed such things the most. Even before finding out about Tom's beard, many of the women in their old town mocked Tom for her masculine features. Sometimes Louisa thought Tom's love of pretty things was to make her look more like a woman and to attain the femininity she never had. Dressing as a man was such a great sacrifice for their family, and both Louisa and Josephine would do well to learn from her example.

By the time the girls had finished baking, the miners had arrived to pick up their clothing. Their house and yard smelled of freshly baked muffins, and as they returned the miners' clothes to them, Louisa couldn't resist giving each one a muffin. There would be less to give to the neighbors, but the light on the miners' faces made it worth it.

A few of them had even given them extra money, thanking them for their kindness and generosity. It brought a lightness to Louisa's heart that would make her next, more difficult task slightly more palatable.

When Jonah arrived home, Louisa gathered the basket of eggs and muffins as well as a loaf of bread they'd been tempted to make and walked over to the neighboring home. Jonah answered the door, looking weary. "What now?"

Shame filled her as she realized just how much she'd hurt the man. Perhaps his sister, too. She wouldn't be kindly disposed to anyone who would hurt one of her sisters.

"I wanted to apologize. I was too harsh with you, and I judged you unfairly. You're right that it's none of my business what goes on in your home. I can only say that my compassion for your children blinded me to my compassion for you and your sister."

She held the basket out to him. "Josephine and I did some baking this afternoon and I would like to share some of the things we made. There's muffins and a loaf of bread, and Josephine kindly offered to share some of our eggs. I hope you will accept our gift and my apology."

He hesitated, so she thrust the basket out again. "Please. You've done so much to be a good neighbor to us, helping us with our home. And I did not repay you with kindness, but with judgment, and for that I am truly sorry."

Nathaniel stuck his head out the door, looking as though he bore no ill effects from his fall. "Miss Louisa. We did our list of chores today, so tonight Papa is going to play the fiddle for us. Are you going to come and sing with us, too?"

She looked up at Jonah, surprised that a worker such as

him would play the fiddle. But again, she chastised herself for her judgment.

"That sounds lovely, if it's not an intrusion. And if it's not too forward, I know it's something my sister and brother would enjoy as well."

Jonah gave a jerk as he nodded. "When Lily was alive, we had neighbors over all the time for such things. But since she died, it hasn't been as much of a priority."

Then he glanced at the basket. "Muffins you say? That must've been the delightful scent I encountered upon arriving home. It was a pleasant surprise, considering the mines and the town don't give off such delightful odors."

His lips curled slightly at the corners. He really was quite handsome when he smiled. But she was not interested in marriage. She still held out hope that once they solved their father's murder, she could find a teaching position somewhere, fulfilling her lifelong dream.

Though she would dearly love a family of her own, she wished to first live the life of the teacher. Though their mother had done an excellent job teaching them at home, the girls also went to school for a brief period of time. And Miss Estes had been a most excellent teacher. She'd given Louisa the courage to believe she could do anything in life, and that the capacity for humankind to achieve anything was limited only by their imagination. She'd particularly enjoyed it when it was her family's turn to board Miss Estes, as she and her mother shared a love of classical literature, which they spent hours discussing.

Even their father had joined in the conversations, and by virtue of such discussions, the girls had developed a love for those things as well. People might not expect that of a farm family, not when there was so much to be done on the ranch. But it was a pleasant way of spending the evenings when it was too dark to work.

Nathaniel tugged at his father's arm. "Please Papa. Tell her they must join us. We could even have dancing."

"No dancing." Jonah's voice was harsh, angry. Then the expression on his face softened. "I haven't danced since their mother died, and it doesn't feel right to do so."

Sympathy for the man filled Louisa's heart. This poor family was grieving the loss of their mother, wife, and perhaps beloved sister-in-law.

"We don't have to dance, if it's too painful for your memory. I know just listening to the music will be enjoyment enough. We used to get together with many of our neighbors as well. This wouldn't be as grand an affair, I don't expect it to be. But I would like for our friendship to grow."

Her heart didn't hurt as much at the memory of their old life as it used to. The parties had ended a few years before their father's death. Too many families had lost their ranches and been forced out by larger operations. She hadn't considered it until now, but Josephine's story about their customer made her realize they were not alone in their tragedy of losing a farm. And as she saw the weary expression on Jonah's face, she was reminded that they were not the only ones to lose a loved one.

Callie came to the door. "What's going on out there? Aunt Clarissa said that supper is waiting, and she's very cross."

Her attempt at doing a good deed had apparently once again backfired. They'd been too long in conversation. Louisa made a motion with the basket. "Perhaps we can do music together another time. Take this and go enjoy your supper. I'm sure we will have many other times when we can all get to know each other. I don't wish to impose upon Clarissa further."

She turned and left, feeling his eyes upon her as she did so. It gave her a strange feeling, being noticed by him. Especially since she didn't know exactly what he thought.

Did he forgive her?

He hadn't said. Would he have agreed with his son's invitation? It was odd how desperately she wanted to know the answers to those questions, considering she had just told herself that romance was out of the question for her. All the same, she still couldn't get him out of her mind.

At least the strange thoughts were hers and hers alone. It was clear Jonah still deeply mourned his wife, and even if she did have any interest in him romantically, she was certain he did not, would not, share her feelings.

CHAPTER 5

*H*e should have done more to be a good neighbor to the Davidson family, considering he'd promised he'd help construct an extra room on their tiny cabin. He'd been thinking a lot about what he wanted, considering the place would eventually become his. But over the past week since his run-in with Louisa, he hadn't taken the time to do so. Which was why, Sunday morning, he felt guilty looking out his window and seeing them working on the house.

As Louisa and Josephine held up a beam while Tom nailed it, he felt even more guilty, watching two women do a man's job. Though the women had helped when they'd fixed up the house and barn to begin with, and he'd been impressed with their strength even then, it still didn't seem right to watch them struggling to get the work done.

But upon closer inspection, he could see that they weren't struggling. The women seemed to be holding the beam with ease, like they were used to such hard work. He supposed they must be, considering they took in laundry, and though it wasn't heavy work, it was still physically demanding. As he opened the door and stepped onto the porch, Louisa stretched. Then she went toward the lumber pile nearby. She picked up a board, and while it didn't appear to be too heavy for her, it was definitely bulky. He often liked having help moving boards of that size, and he was a man.

"Let me help you with that," he said, running toward her.

She gave him a warm smile. "Thank you."

"I'm sorry I haven't had a chance to thank you properly for the lovely goods you sent over. The muffins and bread were delicious, and it was a nice treat to have eggs. I'm sure Clarissa already thanked you, but it would be wrong of me not to do the same."

The pinched look on her face puzzled him. Surely she wasn't angry that he'd taken so long to thank him. He usually relied on Clarissa to do such things, and he had no doubt that she would have done so.

She muttered something under her breath that he couldn't hear, but then smiled at him. "You're very welcome. It was our pleasure and the least we could do."

There wasn't much else to be said, not when she was already lifting the board. Perhaps he'd just misunderstood her expression, and her murmured words had more to do with the fact that the boards they were using were extremely rough cut, and likely full of splinters. For an exterior wall, it would do just fine, but he liked boards that were a little smoother.

"Looks like you need some gloves," he said. "I've got some extra at the house if you'd like."

She shook her head. "That's all right. I have some, but they're too big, and I find it harder to work with them than without. I know it's terribly unladylike, but sometimes we must forgo propriety for the sake of practicality."

Louisa held up a hand. "I'm sure no one will look closely at me to see all the calluses, which can't be helped, given my line of work. And if there is ever a formal occasion here, I do have fancy gloves. It isn't as though I'm trying to attract suitors."

Wasn't that what most women wanted? Considering every time he saw Atherton, the old man mentioned what a lovely wife Louisa would make, it seemed odd that a young lady from a good family wouldn't be looking for a husband. In a town like Blessings, where women were so few, she could have her pick of any man. Not that he was interested. Which he'd told Atherton- several times.

"Surely a young lady such as yourself is looking for marriage and family," he said, smiling.

Louisa shook her head as she lifted her end of the board. "That may be true of many women, but you'd be surprised at how many of us have other aspirations for our lives that don't involve marriage and family."

Her breath caught, and he wasn't sure if it was because of the strain of carrying the board, or because she was upset.

"Certainly, I'd like a family someday," she continued. "But my deepest longing is to be a teacher, helping children the way my teacher, Miss Estes, did. But most schools will only hire unmarried teachers, and therefore, I must remain unmarried until my dream has been fulfilled. I do love children, which is why I spend so much time with yours. It's good practice for when I have a classroom of my own."

They brought the board over to where Tom was waiting with Josephine.

"Nice to see you," Jonah said. "I apologize for not being here sooner to help, but work has kept me busy, and this is the first day off I've had since you moved in."

Tom nodded. "It's the same for me. We don't like working on the Lord's day, but we will have to make up for it later. It's a shame they haven't built a bigger church yet, but I understand they're taking up a collection to do so. We'll be contributing to that as we can, so until then, we have a family service, and do our best to observe as we are able."

Having a decent church built was one of Atherton's pet projects. That, and the school. Did Atherton know of Louisa's aspirations to be a teacher? Atherton had already been discussing plans to build both the school and the church but had told Jonah that they didn't quite have the funds. He'd already been planning on donating his time and some of the materials for the church, so it was nice to hear that another family in town had the same goal.

"Our family does the same," Jonah said. "I've been talking a lot with Atherton about his plans for the church, and while the whole community will be involved in the building of it, I'll be overseeing the project. That is, when we have the funds."

Then he turned and smiled at Louisa. "There are also plans for a school, so if you hadn't yet made it known to Atherton about your desire to become a teacher, I encourage you to speak with him about it. I'll be happy to vouch for your character as someone who is good with children."

That was something he couldn't argue with. He might not have liked her storming into the saloon to chastise him over his son's injuries, but he knew how well she got on with his children. Every day, they'd come home, chattering about Miss Louisa. She must have a special gift with the children, because as much time as they spent with Clarissa, he'd never heard them go on and on about Aunt Clarissa the way they did about Louisa.

Louisa's cheeks tinged pink. "That's a fine compliment, thank you. I would dearly love to teach, and if Blessings were to open a school, I know we could make a good home here."

Josephine nudged her and said something quietly under her breath. Louisa let out a long sigh. Then she said, "That is, if we remain here in Blessings."

Why wouldn't they remain here? The way Atherton talked and acted, he was counting on the Davidson family to form an important part of the community. And with the Davidson siblings contributing to the church, it seemed foolish for them to leave.

"Why wouldn't you stay? Surely in such a short time here, you haven't found this an unpleasant place to live?"

The siblings all looked at one another before Tom answered. "We like it here very much. There's plenty of work, and we have no complaints. But in moving here, we promised Josephine it would be but a temporary stop on our quest to once again have a family ranch."

Josephine's face lit up. "Indeed. It was so good of Atherton to lend us this place to stay, but our animals need more space. Hay is expensive, and I would dearly love for our horses and cows to be able to graze."

A soft expression filled her face. "And I miss having goats. Actually, I miss having a large variety of animals, and I hate having to keep my chickens so cooped up. They like to roam free. At our old house, they were able to do so. But here, if I'm not out, watching them, people try to take them. It will be better for us to have more space and be more isolated."

The siblings exchanged a look he couldn't read, then smiled at him.

"But enough of that," Louisa said. "We still have a long way to go before we have the funds to purchase a new ranch. There are many fine properties around Blessings, and perhaps someday we can afford them. But if they sell before we have the funds, then we'll have to move elsewhere."

Something about the thought of Louisa leaving brought a sinking feeling to his stomach. He didn't want to see them go. Even though he wanted their place for his own, he hated the idea of not looking out his window to see Louisa hanging laundry on the line, humming a tune like no one was watching. He had been watching, and though it was probably wrong of him to do so, he always found himself enchanted by the sight and sound of her. She was a lovely girl.

"You should talk to Atherton about your plans. I know he would be sorry to see you go, and just like he made arrangements to give me the opportunity to eventually purchase this property, perhaps he could preserve one of the ranch areas for you."

Once again, the siblings all looked at each other, then Tom said, "Thank you for the suggestion. We'll take it into consideration. We wouldn't want Atherton to reserve a property for us, preventing someone who could give him money more quickly from having it. If it's in God's will for us to remain here in Blessings, it will all work out. And if God wishes for us to be elsewhere, that way will be shown to us."

He reached for the board they'd brought over. "If you can hold this steady here, I need to attach it to the post."

The area he indicated was much larger than what Jonah had originally envisioned for the building. "What will you do with the space?"

"It will serve as a room for the girls, but as they've been examining the amount of space it takes to dry the laundry outside now, they've realized that come winter, the space we have inside the house won't be sufficient for hanging all the laundry to dry. So even though it is larger than a typical bedroom, it will have a more practical use."

He hadn't thought about winter, but Tom was right. The tiny cabin the three siblings shared would not have enough space for them to run their laundry business in the winter, not when the snow arrived. For a family who didn't know if they were staying in Blessings, they clearly were thinking long-term. Maybe they were just trying not to get their hopes up in case their dream of the perfect property fell through. Even though the Davidsons seemed hesitant to speak with Atherton about reserving some land, perhaps he would have a word with the man about the land, as well as Louisa's hopes for being a teacher. If he gave them enough reasons to stay, then perhaps they wouldn't leave.

Just as quickly as he had that thought, he shook his head.

What was it to him if the family stayed or if they left? Louisa had made it clear that she did not intend to marry, nor did he wish to marry again.

More importantly, why would he be interested in Louisa? True, she had humbled herself and apologized to him for her behavior. But the more he spoke to her and got to know her, the more he realized that her quick tongue and sharp wit wasn't the only unconventional thing about her.

Louisa was nothing like Lily. Unconventional in her ways, he doubted she would be content to spend her days at home with the children, creating a haven for their family.

Not that he would ask Louisa or any other woman to give up her dreams. People needed to be free to be who God created them to be. If Louisa's heart wasn't in having a family, then it wasn't how she should live.

The children ran out of the house, and Jonah smiled.

"Miss Louisa! Papa!"

Their happy cries reminded him of why he worked so hard. Whatever his children wanted to do, he wanted to be there for them. He wanted to enable those dreams.

Clarissa, of course, was nowhere to be seen. She'd been sleeping a lot lately, and when he tried to ask her about it, she snapped at him. He'd asked her several times if she was happy, and if there was anything he could do to make her life easier. But she always told him everything was fine, and that he was worrying too much.

But he did worry.

Though he was grateful for Clarissa's help, there were times when she acted resentful of her role in his home. If he could support her in following her dreams, he would be happy to do so, even though it would come at great expense to his family. He could hire someone, a housekeeper or a nanny, if it meant Clarissa's happiness. But she'd bristled when he'd made the suggestion, the same way she'd bristled when he suggested that perhaps she might like to find a suitor for herself.

He had to wonder if Clarissa had ever really considered what she wanted out of life. Their mother had been an invalid since Clarissa's teen years, and Clarissa had taken care of her well into the time when young ladies were courting and seeking husbands. Then, when their parents died, she'd gotten a job as a clerk at the dry goods store. It was a respectable job, but she hadn't seemed happy. When she'd come to care for his children, he'd thought she was happier, but lately, the same misery he'd detected in her back then had reappeared.

What was wrong with his sister?

The children ran to them, but it wasn't him they greeted first. They threw their arms around Louisa, giving her a warm hug.

"Tell us a story," they said, almost in unison.

Louisa laughed. "I have work to do."

Callie sighed. "You always have work to do."

"I'll tell you what," she said. "You each go find twenty pieces of firewood and stack them in your pile. When you're done, we'll read a bit more from my book."

She had a rather clever way of getting them to do chores. At least now he had a better idea of why their firewood pile had been growing. He'd noticed it earlier in the week, and asked Clarissa about it. She'd said she had no idea where the wood was coming from, so he'd assumed someone had decided to anonymously do a good deed for him, perhaps out of gratitude for him having helped to them with a project.

He'd accepted it as an anonymous gift, knowing that if the giver had wanted to have been made known they would've done so, and were hoping to do the good deeds in private.

But clearly, that wasn't the case.

He looked over the children. "Are you the ones who've been adding to our firewood pile?"

"Yes, Papa." Nathaniel grinned broadly. "Miss Louisa says that it's not right for you to work hard all day and then have to come home and gather firewood in the dark."

When he came home at night, their firewood pile was usually gone, and he only seemed to have time to gather enough wood for the next day, a task that was difficult in the dark. He'd been hoping to find time to gather more wood so that they would have a great deal stockpiled for winter, but so far, he'd worked too long and too hard to be able to do much more than gather what Clarissa would need for cooking. Something about the fact that Louisa had noticed that warmed him to her even more.

He turned to Louisa. "Thank you for being so considerate, and for teaching my children to help out. I'm sure Clarissa would have done so if she weren't busy with everything else, and I'm sure she greatly appreciates you taking an interest in our family."

Though his words honored and respected his sister, he couldn't help feeling a twinge of resentment that Clarissa hadn't thought of such things. Granted, the house did look nicer than it had in a long time, so clearly his discussion with her about doing more with the house had worked. Perhaps it was unfair of him to expect so much of her. She wasn't Lily, who kept the house well organized, spotless, and always seemed to have everything perfectly in order.

"It's no trouble," Louisa said. "The children are often out in the yard, and while I do enjoy their company, I also have work to do. I noticed your wood pile was quite low, and I know how important it is to have a good supply of firewood. When we were children, it was our job to collect the firewood, and since yours are too young to use an axe to split the larger pieces, they've at least brought them close to the house, so you can do so more easily. It's good for them to learn the skills early, as there is so much to be done, and every helping hand counts."

He couldn't tell if that was a criticism of Clarissa or not. He might feel critical of her, but that didn't mean Louisa had the right to be so.

But then she turned and smiled at the children. "Now off you go. The faster you get on with your chores, the faster we can get to our story."

As the children scampered off, Louisa turned back to their pile of lumber. "We're running out of boards again, so come help me get more."

As they walked back to the pile, he said, "It sounds like you do this often with them."

"Every day. When I come out in the morning, it's as though they've been waiting for me, because they immediately burst out of the house, asking for a story. I've had to devise ways of keeping them occupied until lunchtime, otherwise I wouldn't get everything done."

"What do you mean, occupied until lunchtime?"

Louisa lifted her end of the boards, so he took the other end.

"That seems to be when Clarissa rises. Usually around lunch time, she comes to the door in her dressing gown and tells them to come inside. Then I don't see them for the rest of the day."

She sounded as though she were just reporting what she saw, not criticizing, but it bothered him to know that what he thought only happened occasionally was actually something that occurred every day.

Did Clarissa sleep until noon every day? What did his sister get up to, sleeping like that? Every night, she retired early, saying she was exhausted from watching the children. So if she were retiring so early, why would she need to sleep so late?

Surely he didn't have all the facts. He'd been working so much, he barely had time to talk to Clarissa, let alone see the children. He had to take advantage of the good weather to get buildings finished before the cold set in.

They continued working, and when noon approached, sure enough, Clarissa stepped outside. Although not in her dressing gown.

She looked well rested and happy, as she should, sleeping that long.

And then a thought hit him. What if she was ill?

She looked just fine, and her eyes sparkled. He hadn't seen that look on her face in a long time.

"Good morning, Clarissa. I have found the person, or should I say people, responsible for our woodpile. The children have been doing it."

And then he looked around at the neat, tidy yard.

Though the children had clearly been doing this work all week, he hadn't noticed how nice their home looked on the outside until now.

Clarissa looked at them. "Are you sure? I can't get them to do a thing in the house. Why would they gather firewood?"

Louisa smiled. "They just needed the right incentive. We're reading Robinson Crusoe, and the children are just enraptured. However, I will only read to them after they've completed some chores around here. I thought it would be presumptuous of me to ask them to do chores that we need done, so I've been looking around your house, at things they might do to be helpful."

She looked down at the ground and kicked a rock. "Oh

dear, that was probably presumptuous of me as well. I didn't mean to assume about work you needed done, I just did my best to think of what I would've wanted if it were my home. But it's not my home. So, if there are other chores you'd like me to have them do, just tell me. I don't mean to undermine your authority. However, it's the only way I can keep them busy long enough for me to get my own work done."

"It's not presumptuous at all," Jonah said. "I'm grateful for your assistance. I didn't realize my children were bothering you."

Louisa took a step back. "It's no bother, not at all. I enjoy having them around. But as I've said, I do need to get my work done."

He looked over at Clarissa. "Did you know the children were coming over to her house so often?"

Clarissa glared at Louisa. "No, I didn't. I don't know what the children are about, sneaking out like that."

"Sneaking out?" Louisa's voice had taken on a sharp tone. "How can you call it sneaking, when they're quite loud? I would never let them be at my home without permission, so if they shouldn't be out, then you should tell me, rather than accusing us of sneaking. I would never encourage a child to be disobedient."

"They know they're not supposed to leave the yard," Clarissa said.

Callie stepped up to Louisa's side. "We don't leave the yard, just like you told us. There's no fence between our house and Miss Louisa's. Besides, this will be our place someday too, Mr. Atherton said so."

Technically, Callie was right. But it seemed to be bending the rules for her to go over to Louisa's house without permission.

"Did you tell your aunt where you are going to be?" he asked, looking at his children.

"She doesn't like it when we wake her up to ask her things. Besides, she can look out the window and see us plain as day. Anyone can see and hear us from the house. We haven't done anything wrong." Callie stared at him, hands on her hips, like she was commanding a great army.

He looked over at Louisa for confirmation.

"It's true," she said. "Other than that day when Nathaniel fell from the tree, I've had no problems with them. They always do what I ask them, and they never bother me. As I said, my main concern is being able to get our work done."

Clarissa glared at her. "It sounds like you're using them poorly. How do I know you're not making them do chores around your house? I'm sure you're taking advantage of their good nature."

CHAPTER 6

*S*he'd only been trying to do good, but Clarissa was treating her as though she were completely evil. It wasn't right for her to be treated like a criminal, when she'd only been trying to help. Maybe she was wrong for putting the kids to work, but they were all minor chores. Surely, she wasn't so callous as Clarissa was acting.

"I'm dreadfully sorry," she said. "I'd only intended to keep the children gainfully occupied until you were able to take care of them. I didn't think you would see it as taking advantage."

Jonah looked from Louisa to Clarissa, then back to Clarissa, as if he were trying to decide the best course of action. Louisa had already overstepped multiple times with the family and clearly, she was doing it again.

"I do apologize." Louisa clasped her hands in front of her as she smiled at Jonah. "My intention was good. I had only been trying to not be a bother, but I see it causes you concern. If they come to us in the future, I'll leave them to you to deal with. I shouldn't have intervened."

Jonah nodded slowly, his face held a look of uncertainty.

"I don't believe any harm has been done. I'm sure your intentions were good. But if Clarissa is concerned about the activities they do with you, perhaps it is best for you to consult with her first."

Which likely meant the children wouldn't be coming over much at all in the future. Clarissa didn't seem to like her much and, other than her interference, Louisa couldn't understand why. She'd genuinely tried befriending the other woman, but it seemed that the harder Louisa tried, the angrier Clarissa became.

"That sounds good to me," Louisa said, turning to smile at Clarissa. "I do apologize for any offense I might have given. I promise I'll do a better job of consulting you in the future."

The woman gave a smile, but Louisa could see the anger flashing in her eyes. Why did this woman hate her so? It wouldn't do to make an enemy of one's closest neighbor, and, to be honest, didn't wish to make one of someone so beloved to Jonah and the children. For all of her prickliness, it was clear that the family loved Clarissa. Though Louisa hadn't had any conversations with the other woman to find them for herself, surely Clarissa had a good deal of her own good points.

Tom put her hammer down. "We've come up on the noon hour," she said. "Though there is much work to be done, it is important for us to stop and take the time to focus on the Lord."

Tom turned to Jonah. "You and your family are welcome to join us for our noon meal and prayer time. It's nothing as fancy as when the preacher comes for his monthly visits, but we find it good to engage in regular conversation time about the Lord."

Jonah smiled. "That would be welcome indeed. Though I know Clarissa does her best in reading Bible stories to them, it would be good for my children to experience worship with others. While I enjoy my prayer time, I would also enjoy the opportunity for fellowship with another man of God."

A terrified expression crossed Tom's face, Louisa fought the urge to giggle. Everyone believed Tom's deception. If anything, they thought she was a boy, not a woman, pretending to be a man. The lack of feminine features Tom bemoaned back home had become an asset in their quest to find their father's murderer. Though her appearance made their lives easier, sometimes it made Tom's more difficult as many men saw her as a sort of kindred spirit, one who would welcome their confessions and discussion of manly things. Tom had told them that some of them were quite embarrassing indeed.

But Tom quickly recovered her composure and smiled. "Though I am quite close to my sisters," she said. "And we do enjoy our time together, I'm sure having another man's voice in the mix would be welcome."

Then she turned to Clarissa. "And another woman's as well. I find that we all have our own unique experiences and interpretations of life, and everyone has something valuable to contribute. We would love to have you join our group."

Louisa liked that Tom made a concerted effort to include Clarissa. Perhaps Louisa should have been doing that as well. She appreciated her closeness to her sisters for that reason. They often encouraged one another in such things, providing guidance and insight where perhaps the others hadn't been able to see it.

Louisa turned to Clarissa and smiled. "Indeed it would. I must say, I've been longing to get to know you in a deeper way. I would like us to be friends."

The expression on Clarissa's face only darkened. But she smiled, turned to her brother, then said, "If you don't think it would be too much trouble. I don't wish to overexcite the children. Especially on your day off."

Jonah smiled. "It's the perfect way to spend my day off. I believe this would be good rest for us all. And perhaps it will teach the children a little more decorum."

He looked over at the children, who were playing with Zeus. Generally, the rascal wasn't friendly to anyone outside the family. But he seemed to have taken to the children and become their protector as well. Jonah, however, didn't seem to understand this, as his brow was marred with concern.

"Don't worry about them," Josephine said. "I've taught them how to behave around the animals. For someone so small, Nathaniel is especially gifted in dealing with animals."

Jonah nodded. "They've been asking for a dog, actually. But Clarissa says they're too much work. And I don't wish to add to her burdens."

Once again, a defensive expression filled Clarissa's face. But Josephine gave her a kind smile. "You are very wise in saying so. People take on the responsibility of animals, because they want their company. But they don't understand how much work it takes. Unfortunately, too many animals do not get the quality of care they deserve that way. Though the children may not see your wisdom, I am grateful for your foresight."

Josephine's words only made Clarissa's scowl deepen. All any of them wanted to do was befriend this cranky woman, and she seemed to thwart them at every turn.

Louisa brushed her hands on her apron, then turned to her sisters. "We should get our supper ready, and I believe it's a nice afternoon to eat outside. Shall we get the dinner things?"

Jonah looked over at her. "Perhaps we can be of assistance. Is there anything we can do?"

"Yes. Why don't you help the children wash up, and if Clarissa doesn't mind, she could help gather the items we need. Then you and Tom can bring out the table."

Then she thought about the seating arrangement. "Actually, if it's not too much trouble, if you could go to your house, and get chairs for your family, that would be most helpful. We only have four."

There'd been great discussion amongst the sisters about how many chairs to bring, and, for the sake of space, they should have only brought three. But it seemed wrong somehow to not also have their father's chair. There was nothing special about it, since it just looked like all the others. But they still weren't quite ready to say goodbye to him yet.

"I should have thought of that," Jonah said. "The journey to Blessings is difficult, and most people only bring the barest of necessities. It's why business has been so good for me."

His warm smile didn't seem to be particularly directed at her, and yet, she appreciated his open and welcoming demeanor. In some ways it was reassuring, because it made her realize that perhaps she really hadn't done anything wrong, and that Clarissa's coldness was merely a function of her personality.

They all dispersed to their respective jobs. But as Clarissa entered the kitchen, she turned on Louisa.

"I know what you're about," Clarissa said, anger dancing in her eyes. "You might be fooling Jonah with your caring act, but I know your type. You see him as husband material, and you think that by being kind to him and his children, he'll see what a wonderful catch you are and decide to marry you. But let me set the record straight. Jonah was deeply in love with Lily, and he has no intention of ever marrying again. Love that strong is too hard to replace, and he will never see you any as anything more than the woman next door."

At least now Louisa knew the source of Clarissa's rage. Perhaps she feared that if Jonah fell in love, Clarissa would lose her home, or be forced to live with a sister-in-law she couldn't stand.

"Then you have nothing to fear from me. I am not interested in Jonah romantically. Though I'm sure he is a fine man, and I have nothing against him, I do not wish to marry, either. My dream is to become a teacher, and though I would someday love a family of my own, I wish to be a teacher even more. Since most schools require that their teachers be unmarried, it wouldn't be fair for me to give my heart to a man, when my heart is already set firmly elsewhere."

Clarissa looked at her suspiciously, like she didn't quite believe her words.

Louisa smiled. "Truly. I don't know you well, so I don't know what your dreams are for your life. But isn't there something you've wanted, hoped for, that you would do just about anything to get?"

Clarissa didn't answer, but a thoughtful expression filled her face, and it seemed to be devoid of the hostility Louisa was used to.

"You're trying too hard to make us alike, when we are quite different. But I appreciate the gesture. I suppose though, if you truly wish to become a schoolteacher, then you are correct. It would be unwise for you to marry."

Louisa dipped a spoon in the pot of stew that had been simmering on the stove all day and stirred it. Then she opened the oven, pleased to see that the biscuits were nearly browned to perfection. "Would you prefer to carry the biscuits or the stew?"

Clarissa gestured to the pot. "I believe the stew will be easier for me."

Louisa handed her the knitted pads their mother had so lovingly made years ago, when teaching her daughters how to knit. Clarissa picked up the pot and carried it outside, passing Josephine on the way in.

"So she thinks of you as a rival for her brother's affections," Josephine said. "At least that explains things. Though it's a terrible shame that she doesn't see the addition to her family as an enhancement. That is how I would feel if you or Tom were to marry."

Then Josephine looked thoughtful for a moment. "Unless, of course, his first marriage wasn't all that it seemed. Maybe there's more to the story than they're telling. Maybe, when he got married the first time, even though by all accounts she was a lovely woman, she and Clarissa didn't get along."

Though even Clarissa had described Lily as being wonderful, perhaps her sister was right. But it was really none of her concern. Not when she had no designs on Jonah for herself. Hopefully, she could to convince the other woman of that fact.

CHAPTER 7

*E*ven though the families had grown closer as a result of their impromptu Sunday service, Louisa still felt ill at ease around Clarissa. Mostly because Louisa found herself watching the children each morning.

It was almost as if the children were watching for her to come out. Because, like clockwork, as soon as she stepped out the door, the children ran toward her. Most days, they claimed not to have had breakfast and Louisa ended up taking time away from her work to make sure they were fed.

She didn't mind, exactly, except that when Clarissa would poke her head out the door at lunchtime, she'd turn and glower at her.

As Louisa rinsed the final shirt and hung it, she glanced toward their house. Clarissa would be getting up soon. Unlike most days, however, Jonah was walking up the front steps.

She turned to the children. "It looks like your father is here," she said, smiling at them. "He's home early."

The children jumped up from the bench where they'd been sitting, working on their letters.

"Papa," they yelled in unison. They raced toward their father, and it warmed Louisa's heart to see how much they loved him.

And clearly, by the way he swung them up in his arms, he felt the same way. Surely he wouldn't approve of them running wild all day.

She couldn't hear what they said to him, but afterwards, he turned and looked in her direction. The expression on his face warmed her, and she found the silly urge to giggle.

What was wrong with her? It was just a friendly greeting from a neighbor. And yet, she felt all giddy and giggly inside.

Callie said something to him, then he turned and looked over and walked in her direction. Louisa wiped her hands on her apron and smiled at him. "Good afternoon Jonah. It's so nice to see you. What brings you home so early?"

Jonah frowned. "Some of the supplies I needed were due on the next freight, but they haven't shown up yet. The freight is late. I thought I'd come home for lunch, maybe do some work around the house that's been neglected. What are the children doing here? Where is Clarissa?"

This was it. Her opportunity to let him know what was going on. And yet, she struggled to come up with the words. Was it right to put down the other woman? Of course, she didn't necessarily have to give an opinion on the matter, just state the facts.

"I'm afraid I don't see her much. The children often come out to play without her. They were just working on some lessons I'd given them, but as you can see, I've got work to do, so I was trying to combine my work with a few school lessons."

He looked at her like he couldn't comprehend her words.

"Clarissa should be watching them. I'm sure you're mistaken. She told me herself that the situation was under control."

She wasn't mistaken, but it seemed that to argue her point further would only malign Clarissa.

As if on cue, Clarissa stepped out of the house, carrying a bucket.

"Hello, Jonah. I wasn't expecting you home so soon. The children and I were just off to get some water." Clarissa sent Louisa a glare.

Had the other woman overheard her mention the time she spent with the children?

Louisa hadn't said anything untruthful, so she didn't like the way Clarissa looked at her like she'd committed a crime. The only crime here was that Louisa was taking away precious time needed to help Josephine to help Clarissa instead.

"Very good," Jonah said, putting down Nathaniel. "I'm sure you've got quite a lot planned, so I'll do my best to stay out of your way."

She couldn't read the look he sent her, and she didn't think it was a complimentary one. Not knowing what else to do, she smiled at them both. "Well, it was nice seeing all of you. But we have a rather large order to take care of today, so I'd best be getting back to work."

She thought she heard Clarissa mutter something about finally minding her own business, but she couldn't be certain enough to confront her on it. Louisa would be more than happy to mind her own business, if two active children weren't constantly inserting themselves into it.

As she turned to leave, she could feel Jonah's eyes on her, studying her, like he didn't understand why she would lie. And why would she? But that would mean he'd have to figure out what his sister was up to, and he didn't seem willing to look deeper.

Fine by her.

But it would be nice to get some acknowledgement for

the amount of time she spent with the Hastings children, even if it was just a simple thank you.

At least it was preparation for becoming a teacher. She'd been told it was a thankless job, but working with the children was reward enough. And, as she glanced over her shoulder at Jonah's children, Callie smiled at her and waved. Yes, it was rewarding spending time with Nathaniel and Callie. She just hated that it always left her feeling like she'd done something wrong.

JONAH HAD HOPED THAT, by befriending his neighbors, it would make relations easier between the two families. Not that he had any problems with them. But it seemed like things were not well with Clarissa. She pretended like nothing was wrong, but he saw the way she scowled every time he mentioned Louisa.

Were the children misbehaving again? Was Louisa just not telling him?

He'd asked her to back off, if only for Clarissa's sake. But it seemed like, even though outwardly everything looked fine, there remained tension that didn't seem to have an explanation. He'd asked the children how things were, but they gave him the same answer. Everything was fine. But the expressions on their faces told him that wasn't true.

Which was why, when they went to get water, he didn't feel too guilty taking a peek into Clarissa's room. Was she, as Louisa claimed, always in bed until afternoon?

Her bedclothes were rumpled, but that wasn't necessarily a sign she'd been in bed all day. Clarissa wasn't the best housekeeper. He was starting to think that maybe his suspicion that something was wrong was all in his head.

However, as he turned to leave Clarissa's room, he

tripped over a pile of dirty clothes, and a bottle rolled out from under them. His heart sank as he recognized the bottle. Spirits, which he expressly forbade having in his home. His father had been an alcoholic, drinking too much, and making their life miserable because of it. He had been a lazy, self-absorbed man, who was often fired from his job for either not showing up to work on time or showing up drunk.

All their lives, Jonah and Clarissa promised that they would not be like their father. And yet, suddenly, it all made sense. Clarissa's anger, her moodiness, her lying abed until noon, and even the children's secrecy. Growing up, they'd learned to keep their father's secrets at the risk of facing the wrath of his belt.

How had Jonah been so blind? He'd thought that his children would be safe with his sister. Clarissa of all people would understand the dangers of the devil drink. He picked up the bottle and carried it out into the other room. He had to confront her. But how? And when? And what was he supposed to do about the children?

Before he could even ponder the answers to those questions, a ruckus in the yard startled him. Clarissa was screaming at Louisa.

"I told you to stop interfering. How dare you encourage the children to violate my rules?"

Jonah went outside to see Louisa standing in the yard, her arm around the children, Clarissa facing her, looking angrier than a nest of hornets that had been roused.

"If you were watching them properly, it wouldn't have happened. You get angry with me if I wake you up because the children are disturbing me, and you also get angry with me for keeping them occupied. Nothing I do is right when it comes to you, but you're forgetting that there are two children who desperately need guidance."

Tears were streaming down Louisa's face. Jonah stepped

around the house and into view. Louisa shrank back and pointed the children in his direction. "Go to your father."

He didn't have the full story, and though he was angry with Clarissa, he owed it to her, the children, and even Louisa, to find out before he made any assumptions.

"What's going on here?"

Clarissa stepped forward. "The children disappeared when my back was turned. As many times as I have told them not to go next door, and not to bother Louisa, they did so anyway. And despite the fact that I have told Louisa countless times not to entertain the children, the children just told me that they had lunch at Louisa's earlier."

Louisa looked at him apologetically. "I could hear their stomachs rumbling. We were having our noon meal anyway, and the children said they hadn't even had breakfast. They told me Clarissa was asleep and she told them not to disturb her. I did what I thought was best, and I'm sorry if that's wrong. But I cannot deny food to a hungry child."

How could he fault her? True, he could see where Clarissa had asked her not to interfere with her care of the children. Had it been him, he would've done the same thing. Plus, now that he'd found the empty bottle of liquor, he wasn't sure how much of Clarissa's story he could believe anymore.

"It was very generous of you to make sure my children had lunch," he said, smiling at Louisa. "Perhaps we can all discuss a more rational solution. But first, I think I must have a private word with my sister. Would it be a terrible imposition to ask you to watch my children for just a little while longer?"

Louisa nodded slowly, like she wasn't sure about accepting when she knew it would anger Clarissa. "Certainly. And if the two of you haven't eaten either, I'm sure we have some food left."

Given the circumstances, she was being incredibly decent

about it. He just wished he understood what was going on with his sister. And he prayed that the situation wouldn't be as devastating as it had been with his father.

"That sounds wonderful, thank you. I appreciate your generosity."

Clarissa looked livid at his words, her eyes flashing the way they did when she was being thwarted. Why should she care if the neighbor woman wanted to help the children? Especially if she was fighting a battle with the bottle.

They went inside, and as soon as the door closed behind them, Clarissa turned on him. "How dare you interfere. You had no right going against me. Now, the children will think they don't have to listen to me because you just contradicted me in front of them."

"I'm more concerned about this," he said, reaching for the bottle he'd found in her room.

"Where did you get that?"

He looked down at the bottle, then back at her. "You know where I got it. The question is, why was it there?"

"You had no right going through my things," she said, reaching for the bottle. "This is none of your concern."

He stared at her. "How can you say this is none of my concern? After what we went through with our father?"

She wrenched the bottle from his grasp. "This is nothing like that. You don't know what you're talking about."

"Don't I? All the secrecy? The strange way both you and the children have been behaving? And what about Louisa's claims that you sleep until well past noon? Tell me the truth."

He was so angry his hands were shaking. He hadn't felt that way in a long time. Not since Lily had died in childbirth. He'd gone for the doctor, and the doctor had told him there was plenty of time, that Jonah was being overly worried for no reason. The doctor hadn't come, and the baby was turned the wrong way. Both Lily and the baby had died before the doctor had gotten there. Jonah never done physical violence to anyone, not even the doctor on that day, when he had lost the woman dearest to him and a child they'd longed for. He had that same feeling now.

He hated staring at his sister, knowing she wasn't telling the truth and hating that someone he loved so much could be so deceitful.

"You wouldn't understand," she said.

"What I don't understand is that Louisa has been claiming you're neglecting my children, and you've been denying it, calling her a liar. And yet, I find evidence of a very likely reason why you are neglecting them. So, tell me what's really going on, or else."

He didn't know what the "or else" would be, but he prayed it wouldn't come to that. He loved Clarissa so much. Why couldn't she have confided in him? Did she understand that these were his children at stake? It wasn't fair to have the dearest people in his life pitted against each other.

"Or else what?" The anger on her face made him feel even deeper betrayal.

Jonah gestured to one of the chairs. "I can't comprehend what's going on. I love you too much to threaten anything terrible, but I'm genuinely worried. Let's talk about this more rationally, and whatever it is, I will help you. There is nothing so shameful you can't tell me about it. But you have to tell me everything, and it has to be the truth"

Clarissa sat in the chair he indicated as tears ran down her face. "But that's just it. It's so shameful, I fear you'll force me from the house, and I'll never see you or the children again."

His heart was filled with compassion for the woman he so dearly loved. "There is nothing so shameful. Jesus did not cast stones at the sinful woman, and I know whatever's going on is not so bad as that. So, tell me. I was wrong to yell at you the way I did, but I let my emotions take over."

Clarissa looked down at the bottle. "I only have one sip. At the beginning of the night, and at the end of the night, to loosen my vocal chords. Back when I worked at the shop, one of our customers was a singing master, and he liked my voice. Sometimes, he would meet me and teach me."

He stared at her. "You told me you had no suitors. Please tell me you did not give up your chance of love for me."

Clarissa laughed and shook her head. "No. He was an old man, past his prime. I loved singing, and he taught me many things about how to maximize my voice. One of his tips was to take a sip of whiskey before and after I sang to help my vocal chords."

A peaceful expression crossed her face as she spoke about her singing, but that didn't explain why she was drinking now.

"But what about now? You refuse to sing with us, so how is it that you would need whiskey to help your voice?"

She gave a soft smile. "A few months ago, when I was doing the wash, Ellie Baines, who owns the saloon, heard me singing. she said I had the most beautiful voice she'd ever heard. Talking to her was like speaking to my singing teacher."

He'd never seen his sister look so happy. Her face took on an almost blissful expression, despite the seriousness of their discussion, as she continued her story.

"She invited me to sing in the saloon. I wear a disguise, so no one will know who I am, but I'm afraid someone will recognize my voice if I sing elsewhere. It would be disgraceful to you and the family if anyone finds out. Everyone thinks the girls singing in the saloon are loose women."

He hadn't expected this to be her secret. True, singing in

the saloon wasn't a respectable activity for a woman like Clarissa, who was from a good family. But it also wasn't so unforgivable that he would be ashamed of her.

Jonah stared at her, trying to puzzle her out. "How do you make it work? I never hear you coming, going, or notice you gone."

She shrugged. "You spend evenings in your workshop and you sleep soundly. It's not difficult to leave in the middle of the night. I don't sing until late, and when I'm finished, I return home, and go to bed so it's like I never left."

Clarissa looked down at her hands. "I do sleep in. I've tried getting up with the children and doing everything I need to do in the morning, but it's so difficult."

Then she returned her attention to him. "I was just afraid that if I admitted to sleeping in, you would think I was ill. I know I was wrong, especially because I made it out to be that Louisa was a liar, but I thought the truth was more shameful. Even now, I'm afraid to admit to her why I am out so late and must sleep late to catch up. The days I don't sleep in, my voice is terrible at night, and even though it's not in the best situation, I truly enjoy the singing."

Singing in the saloon wasn't the life he'd have wanted for her but when she spoke about it, it looked as though the happiness she'd been missing from her life had returned. She was the girl Jonah remembered, had grown up with, so how could he hold it against her?

Suddenly, his family problems didn't seem so simple after all. He'd always thought Clarissa could be a famous singer. But those plans didn't include singing in the saloon of some gold mining town, cavorting with the roughest of the rough.

He examined his sister's face, looking for any sign that the situation wasn't what it seemed. "I've heard the saloon is rough at night. Do the men harass you?"

She shook her head. "No. Ellie makes sure of it. She

doesn't want anyone bothering me. She's a woman just like me, trying to make her way in a situation that's not always friendly to women. I've made it clear that I'm a good girl, and I have no intention of participating in any other activities. I'm there to sing, nothing more."

Even though Clarissa had told him so many lies these past few weeks, he believed her. Looking at her now, with the pretense that had been between them gone, there was a raw honesty to her face.

"You feel safe there?"

Clarissa nodded. "I do. Like I said, Ellie makes sure of it. So many people come to hear me sing that she doesn't want to ruin business by having me quit."

Still, it was almost unbelievable. "How could I have not known? How do people not recognize you?"

She smiled. "I wear a wig. No one would suspect that someone like me, an ordinary woman with mousy brown hair would turn into a siren with bright blonde hair. And, Ellie is the only one who knows. I use a stage name, The Songbird of the West."

The name did sound familiar. He'd seen advertisements for The Songbird of the West, and he'd heard many men discuss their enjoyment of her singing. He'd often thought he'd like to hear her perform, except that it would be completely improper for him to do so. A widower like himself, with the family to think of, did not spend time in saloons listening to women sing.

"Why have you refused to sing with us as a family?"

She gave a slight shrug. "One day, when I was doing the wash, a man overheard me singing. He told me I sounded just like The Songbird and wanted to know if we were related. He was so demanding in his questions that it really shook me up. I told him that I was not, and I knew of no such creature. I managed to get him to leave, but ever since then,

I've been afraid to sing at home. What if someone else recognizes me and refuses to buy my excuses?"

He hadn't thought of that, and though they were hostile at first, he could see now that her answers were forthcoming, like she was happy to finally tell him the truth about her secret.

"I wish you would have just told me. We would have found a way to work it out."

"Then you approve of my singing in the saloon at night?"

He shrugged. "It wasn't my first choice of careers for you, but I have to say that I'm deeply relieved. I was fearful that there was something wrong with you."

But suddenly, relief over Clarissa's situation was replaced by worry for his children. "Still, there remains the question of the children. Now that I know why you sleep in, I don't feel that it's right for you to watch them until you've had your rest. They can be trying in our best moments, but with little sleep, I can see why you've had so many difficulties."

Clarissa looked defeated. "I know. I do my best by them, I really do."

He glanced out the window, where Louisa was playing some sort of game with the children. "Why won't you just let Louisa watch them? Why are you so angry with her all the time? It seems to me that she would very willingly care for them, especially if she knew the circumstances."

"The circumstances?" Clarissa shook her head. "A respectable, God-fearing family approving of my singing in the saloon? You heard her in prayer. The whole family is so dignified, so focused on serving God, I fear they would judge ordinary people like us for not being as holy as them."

Jonah shook his head. "I disagree. They have a deep love of God, yes, but it's more than that. They live their lives out of a love of God, not of judgment."

He thought back to a couple of weeks ago when Louisa

had come with her apology. "I know Louisa acts judgmental sometimes, but that day, when she brought over a basket of goods for us, she was genuine in her regret over having judged us. Since then, I've seen her working very hard to understand rather than judge. Perhaps if we gave her a chance, she would understand."

Clarissa groaned. "That's just because she's hoping to sink her claws into you. I'm sure what she really wants is to make you think she's loving and kind, but as soon as your back is turned, she'll be the first to stick her claws into it."

"Why would you think that? I know she's not as wonderful as Lily was, but Louisa would make any man a fine wife. Not that either of us are interested. You seem to think there's a romance brewing between us, but I can assure you that is the furthest thing from the truth. Louisa has confided in me a deep dream of becoming a schoolteacher. If she marries, most school boards wouldn't hire her."

Clarissa gave a harsh laugh. "So much you know. Lily wasn't the angel you thought she was. I know it's wrong to speak ill of the dead, but you needn't worry about someone not living up to her greatness. When you weren't around, she was cruel. Always mocking me for not being as pretty and clever as she was. She told me I'd never get myself such a great husband as she did. She and her friends used to laugh at me behind their fans, making me the butt of their jokes. She was not a nice woman, only to you."

He'd have said his sister was lying, but he could see the pain in her eyes. "Why didn't you tell me?"

"Who am I to stand between a man and his wife? I'd always hoped that you would see with your own eyes, but yours were too busy mooning over her. And it doesn't matter now. Lily is gone, and even though she was unkind to me, I am grateful for how well she loved you. I know you were happy with her, and that's what matters.

The largest issue, was, of course, his children. And even though Clarissa had ill feelings toward his late wife, he didn't believe they reflected on Louisa.

"Was Louisa ever unkind to you? When I wasn't around?"

The fighting look was back on Clarissa's face, but then she shook her head. "I will admit that, other than our scuffles over the children, she has been nothing but kind."

Then Clarissa let out a long sigh. "I would have to say that, even though I've been harsh with her, she hasn't responded in kind. I suppose I owe her an apology, but it's infuriating that she seems to interfere every turn I make."

"But I thought it was only because you weren't there. What's really your problem with Louisa?"

Clarissa let out a long sigh. "I suppose mostly it's that I'm afraid she'll find out my secrets. If you knew that I slept until noon every day, you would ask questions, just as you're doing now. I didn't think you would respond favorably."

Then she looked out the window, a longing expression on her face. "I know it isn't one of the grand opera houses, but I have very much enjoyed singing again. I know it sounds foolish, and prideful, but I have rather enjoyed having people pay so much attention to me. To give me so much applause."

She'd spent so much of her life caring for their invalid mother. When she died, Jonah had offered Clarissa a home with him and Lily. He'd thought she was going to accept, but then she proudly told him she'd found a job at the mercantile and was going to be an independent woman.

"You didn't take that job because you wanted to be independent, did you? You wanted to be away from Lily."

She nodded slowly, looking regretful. "You were newly married, and so happy. But Lily told me it would ruin everything if I moved in with you. She was the one who helped me get my job."

How had he been so blind to all of this? But, he supposed

he had been too in love to look deeper. And, the times he did question Lily about things that didn't seem right, she told him he was being silly and would do something to prove him wrong.

"Once I started working, socializing was difficult for me. I was too tired at the end of the day. And then, when you would convince me to go out with you and Lily, I had to listen to Lily and her friends making snide remarks about me. Lily was always jealous of my singing, and she liked to tell people that I was too prideful about my voice, that I was showing it off because I had no other good qualities."

Even though it was a sad story, he couldn't help smiling at his sister's description. A barn cat on the prowl had better pitch than Lily, and no one appreciated it when she sang. Not even Jonah, and he was in love with her.

"I never realized she was jealous of your singing. But now that you mention it, I do remember her making comments about wishing you didn't show off. At the time, I attributed it to her modesty, but now I see it was jealousy. I'm so sorry. Can you forgive me?"

Clarissa nodded. "Only if you can forgive me for these past few months. I honestly thought I could do it all. But I can't. It's no wonder Louisa would forego having a family in order to become a schoolteacher. Once you find your life calling, it consumes you. And trying to do other things, like caring for people, is exhausting."

At least Clarissa was starting to sound sympathetic. But that still left them with the question of the children.

"Perhaps we can make an arrangement with her to have her give the children lessons in the mornings. I would pay her, of course, and not just because I feel that the children should be cared for."

The more he thought about it, the more it made sense. She was already teaching the children things. And though

Clarissa cared for the children, they'd never set out any expectation of her teaching them. It was time both children began learning lessons.

"Without a school in Blessings, and the children needing to learn, it seems reasonable to me that we would ask Louisa to take on that position until she can find one of her own."

The dejected look returned to Clarissa's face. "Yes, but that means I'm going to have to humble myself to her."

"Given the many times she's humbled herself to me, I can't see that she would be unreasonable towards you. Give her a chance. You've been blinded by your experience with Lily and your fear of your secret being discovered, so you haven't taken the time to see her for who she really is."

He gave her a warm smile. "And even though you feel she has something against you, I believe she is a warm enough woman that she will give you a chance. Not just about the children, but with your singing as well. I cannot lie to them about why we need the children to be taken care of. I'm sure they will practice the utmost amount of discretion, but we cannot expect them to do a favor for us without being open with them."

At Clarissa's nod, he should have felt elated. But he knew that was only half the battle. He had to convince Louisa to do the job. She'd obviously been doing it on her own, but that didn't mean she would want to formalize things.

He glanced out the window again. Clarissa came up behind him. "Are you sure you aren't developing feelings for her? You seem very intent on defending her character. And you sound rather certain of her finer qualities."

He turned to look at her. "It doesn't matter. She's not inclined to marry, and I'm not inclined to prevent a woman from following her dreams. Having seen her with the children, I know she would be a wonderful teacher. I cannot imagine others being denied the pleasure of such an experience."

As Clarissa continued to stare at him in a knowing way, he shook his head. "Besides, I've just found out that the wife I thought was a wonderful, kind, caring woman had been most unkind to someone I dearly love. How do I know that Louisa, or any other woman, won't be the same?"

Clarissa nodded. "We all have our secrets. That shouldn't deter you. But you are wise in taking time to assess a person's character more deeply before deciding yourself in love. Still, I think it would be wrong if you do not consider remarriage or finding love again if that is where God takes you."

He chuckled. "God? And here you were just fearing the judgment of people who would quote God in their response."

Clarissa shrugged. "I do try to live a godly life. And I will admit that I feel much better now that I'm no longer lying to you. At first, I was constantly praying and apologizing to God for my deception. But I knew my words meant nothing as long as I continued deceiving you. Now, I believe I can be more open with God and less hypocritical. If you are right about Louisa and her sisters, it will be good to have their example."

CHAPTER 8

*W*hen Jonah and Clarissa came out of the house, the children hung back.

"I'm afraid Auntie will be very cross with me," Callie said. "I was supposed to wake her up if Papa came home early."

Louisa wasn't so sure. From the newly relaxed demeanor between Clarissa and Jonah as they walked toward them, Louisa had to think that whatever problem had been between them had been resolved. The children, however, did not. Nathaniel clung to her skirts, and Callie stayed hidden behind her.

"Children, you needn't be afraid," she said. "You know your father loves you."

"Auntie is very cross with us," Callie said again. Louisa nudged the little girl. "Look at her face. Does she look cross to you?"

Indeed, there was a brighter smile on Clarissa's face than Louisa had ever seen. The woman looked happier than anyone had a right to be happy. Perhaps she had a secret beau and had just confessed to her brother.

An odd thing to think. She didn't know Clarissa, but she

had the look of a woman in love. Strange to think of being in love, but the closer Jonah came, the more her heart twisted in a funny way.

She liked Jonah. Maybe even more than liked him, but she couldn't say for certain.

She didn't have much experience in that area, since none of the men back home had ever tempted her. Not that any of them had been interested.

Men didn't like smart women, as the women in town had often taunted her. As much attention had been made to the way Tom didn't fit in, the truth was, none of the sisters did. Josephine, with her deep love of animals, and Louisa, with her deep love of books, were both seen as oddities.

And even though Louisa felt that funny feeling in the pit of her stomach- a mixture of excitement and terror- she knew Jonah would never feel the same way. Clarissa had made it quite clear that his heart had been firmly buried with his wife.

Which should have been just fine with Louisa, because a romance at this point in her life would be absolutely ridiculous. It would ruin everything she'd worked so hard for.

But as she turned her gaze to the tiny town emerging in the shadows of the hills, she couldn't imagine being any further from her dream.

Hopefully, they would find information on her father's murderer soon, and then she could begin writing letters and answering advertisements for schoolteachers. Then, she looked down at her hands, and realized it might be a little longer before her hands would be healed enough to be seen as a proper lady. They were so raw now, that even gloves didn't slide on them smoothly. She and Josephine had taken to sleeping with their hands slathered in the salve Kela Tukumu, one of the women from the nearby Miwok tribe, had traded her for.

Living so close to the river, the Davidson family occasionally had contact with the Miwoks living on the other side. Josephine was becoming friends with Kela, who was learning to become a medicine woman. Though the salve Kela made worked, and their hands were getting better, it didn't help that they were still doing laundry.

But none of that mattered. They were still too far from accomplishing what they'd set out to do, which meant thinking such thoughts about a man were totally improper.

"Children? Why are you hiding behind Louisa?" Jonah's voice was firm but confused. After their happy and hearty greeting earlier, it was no wonder he was surprised.

"They're afraid that you'll be cross that Clarissa is upset with them. But as I explained to them, Clarissa looked quite happy, not upset."

Louisa smiled at Clarissa, hoping the other woman would see that she was on her side. Even though all her other attempts to befriend the woman had backfired, she still held out hope that someday, they could be friends. Or, if not friends, at least pleasant acquaintances.

"I'm not upset," Clarissa said. "I'm glad Jonah came home early today, because it gave us a chance to talk about things that were important to us."

She squatted down near Nathaniel. "I'm sorry I made you afraid of me. I know I yelled at you a lot, and I shouldn't have. I was just very tired, and when I'm tired, sometimes I say or do things that are wrong. But your father and I have spoken, and we've come to an agreement that will allow me to sleep more, and then I won't be so cross."

Nathaniel loosened his hold on her skirts. Callie stepped forward. The children were still tense, like they weren't sure what to make of Clarissa's apology. It wasn't often an adult apologized to children, so Louisa could understand her hesitation.

"You should tell her you accept her apology," Louisa said gently, nudging Callie.

"How do I know you mean it?" Callie asked.

Jonah stepped forward. "Because she apologized to me, and I accepted her apology. Things are going to change around here, and there's still much for the adults to discuss, but I'm hoping we can make things better for everyone."

The children ran to their father and threw their arms around him. Clarissa slowly stood, looking hurt that they hadn't acknowledged her. Louisa gave her a smile.

"Don't mind them. When their father is around, I've noticed they only have eyes for him."

Clarissa nodded slowly. "I don't suppose I've done myself any favors with how I've acted lately."

Clarissa had mentioned being tired and needing sleep. As Louisa examined the other woman's face, she wondered if perhaps Clarissa might be ill and hiding it, and finally confessed as much to Jonah.

"When we're not at our best, sometimes we do things we regret. I'm sure the children will forgive you. Children seem to have an openness toward forgiveness that many adults lack."

Clarissa chuckled. "You don't know them well at all, do you? I've never seen a bigger grudge holder than Callie. She still reminds me of the time when she was three years old and she'd gotten herself stuck in a tree, so I told her to jump and I would catch her, only the force of her fall pushed us both to the ground. She wasn't injured, but she cited it as evidence that I didn't keep my word and catch her."

Clarissa chuckled, and once again, Louisa saw the glimmer of someone who wasn't nearly as unpleasant as she'd once thought her to be.

Callie walked over to them. "Well you didn't catch me. I

landed on the ground. And who says I wasn't injured? I tore my favorite dress."

Jonah, who had picked up Nathaniel and was holding him in his arms, laughed. "Your dress was torn on the tree. And while she didn't catch you in the literal sense, she did break your fall, saving you from injury. As I recall, Clarissa suffered a nasty scrape from landing on a rock."

The little girl lifted her head the way she did when she was being stubborn. "Mama used to say that it was proof that she didn't know anything about children."

Clarissa and Jonah exchanged a glance that made Louisa feel like an intruder. But she didn't like the way the little girl was looking at her aunt, so she said, "I'm sure you misunderstood what your mother meant. Your aunt does a wonderful job of caring for you, and she deserves much more of your respect."

Whatever moment happened between Jonah and Clarissa passed as Louisa spoke, and Clarissa's shoulders softened. "That's kind of you to say," she said. "But you've taken me to task many times for not watching over them properly."

And yet, judging by the attention and the other woman's voice, even though Clarissa was making an admission Louisa had long hoped to hear, it didn't feel good to her. She'd never meant to break the other woman. Especially since it sounded like Callie's mother had made comments about Clarissa to the children. Clarissa must think everyone was her enemy. No wonder she was so bristly around Louisa.

"And as I've said many times, I'm sure I don't understand everything in your family. Jonah is a wonderful father who clearly loves his children, and I know he would never put them in a situation where he felt they were unsafe. I feel very badly for having judged you, and I hope someday we can move past that disagreement."

Clarissa shook her head. "No. Please. Allow me to apologize. You're right. I wasn't watching them in the mornings. I stay up very late, and I'm too exhausted in the mornings to get up and care for them properly. I tried giving them rules to follow to stay in the house and not cause any trouble, but they never listen. And though I've tried to keep my need for sleep secret, it has been discovered, and it's time I owned up to my wrong actions."

Josephine came around the house, carrying a basket of laundry she had just taken off the line. "Hello. I didn't realize we had visitors. I could put the kettle on."

Louisa chuckled. They always had the kettle on. They had to for the laundry. But her sister was being polite, and she appreciated it.

Jonah shook his head. "I don't believe that's necessary. But I was wondering if I might impose upon you to keep the children occupied while my sister and I have a word with Louisa."

Josephine looked at Louisa, like she was afraid of what the conversation might entail. Considering how many times Josephine has chastised Louisa for her unkindness toward Clarissa and her disagreements with how the children were being treated, it was no wonder. But after Clarissa's apology, Louisa sensed there was something different about this conversation.

"It's all right. We won't be long," Louisa said. She walked with them to the small garden behind their house, if one could call it a garden. There weren't many flowers, but there was a rather pleasant sitting bench, and as they walked over, Louisa noticed that another bench had been added. "Is this new?"

Jonah nodded. "I love building furniture, and it suits me in the evenings after the children have gone to sleep to do something with my hands."

She looked over at him and realized that he must be

suffering from a deep loneliness indeed, having lost his wife. The vulnerability in his voice reminded her that those little butterflies she felt in her stomach were hers and hers alone. How could he ever give his heart to anyone else?

When Louisa sat on the bench, she was surprised to find that Clarissa sat next to her. She'd assumed that she'd sit on the other bench with her brother.

Clarissa looked at her sheepishly, and said, "I realize I haven't been very kind to you, and for that I am dreadfully sorry. I was afraid that if we spoke too much, I would tell you too many of my secrets."

Then Clarissa shook her head. "No, I wouldn't have told you. It would have led you to asking questions, and you already questioned me too much. I didn't want Jonah to figure out what was going on."

Clarissa looked over at Jonah, who seemed to already know what his sister was going to say. Louisa smiled at her. "It's all right, you can tell me."

But Clarissa looked embarrassed. "I'm just afraid of what you'll think of me. I know you already think I'm a terrible person, based on the poor care I take of the children, but I'm afraid this will only make it worse."

Josephine was right to take her to task for her judgmental attitude. After all, she had been wrong in judging the other woman. But now, with the way Clarissa seemed afraid to confide in her, she could understand the deeper impact judging others had. When it was time for them to be open with you, or if they needed to be, they couldn't.

"I was wrong to do so," Louisa assured her. "I'm working on that. It's one of the things I pray about every day. I obviously still have a long way to go, given your fear of me, and for that I am truly sorry. But none of us are without our secrets, and if this is one that you share with me, you needn't fear unburdening yourself. I am in no place to judge."

Jonah smiled at her in a way that warmed her far too much to be proper. Then he looked over at Clarissa. "See? I told you we could trust her."

His faith in her gave her more encouragement than she would have liked. Once again, she was putting too much stock in this man and his opinion of her. And though his compliment was a fine one indeed, part of her wanted to tell him it wasn't necessary. But she sensed that if she tried, he would only compliment her further, making things even more awkward. So instead she turned to Clarissa and took the other woman's hands.

"Do not be afraid. I cannot imagine it would be anything so shameful that I would not understand. Not because I am so good, but because I know the deep love of the Lord. Who among us is to cast stones?"

Clarissa squeezed her hand. "I know you're trying to encourage me with your words of wisdom from the Lord. But that is exactly why I fear telling you. Churchgoing folks would be horrified."

"Then it is only because they have not dealt with their own sin. I've found that most judgment from others is more about them being unwilling to face their own sin then it is about your sin." Louisa gave Clarissa's hands another squeeze and stood. "Look at me. What do you see?"

Clarissa gave her a funny look, so Louisa smoothed her skirts, and smiled at the other woman. "I'll tell you what the people in our former town saw. I was smart, educated. And though my household valued those qualities, many people found it unseemly for a woman to love books as much as I do. No one could understand why I would prefer to be a teacher over doing what everyone else did: marrying and having children. Everyone thought that I would do well to marry the blacksmith's son, who would have been able to provide me with a roof over my head and food in my belly.

But he was a vile man, unkind to women, children, and animals. Why is that lucky? As a teacher, I could put my own roof over my own head, and do something I love, with people I love. But in those people's minds, marrying a man I didn't love would have been a better life for me."

She glanced back at her house, thinking of Tom's shame. She wouldn't reveal her sister's secret to them, because it wasn't her secret to tell. But when she turned her attention back to Clarissa, she smiled again.

"What I have come to realize, is that their dislike of me and my choices was because they hadn't made better choices for themselves. None of those women were married to men they loved. My mother used to tell me that a marriage for love is a wonderful and mysterious thing, very rare, and something to be treasured."

She turned to look over at Jonah. "The way your brother speaks of his late wife, he must have had that. For that, I am glad. But all those miserable women, judging me because I wouldn't make the same choices, they weren't criticizing me because I was making a bad decision. No, they were jealous of my strength in choosing a life I wanted, rather than one forced upon me."

Suddenly, their decision to come to Blessings felt like the best decision she'd ever made. Until speaking with Clarissa, she hadn't realized just how unhappy she was in their old social circle, with the women who twittered behind their fans about the crazy Montgomery sisters.

"I have a dream," Clarissa said quietly. "I think that's what bothered me so much when you spoke of becoming a school-teacher. Yours is at least possible. I wasn't sure how to make mine a reality, which is part of my secret."

Jonah got up from his bench and walked around behind Clarissa, putting his hands on her shoulders. "But your dream is important to me, just as Louisa's is. I'll support you however I can in achieving your dream."

Then he looked up at Louisa. "And that's why we wanted to talk to you. Though Clarissa isn't exactly doing what she always dreamed of, it's close. And it's the best we can do for her for now. I didn't know it until today, and yet the more I think about my sister's passion, the more I believe it would be wrong to deny her."

What on earth were they talking about?

Louisa looked over at Clarissa. "And what is this dream of yours? Does it have something to do with what you're ashamed to tell me?"

Clarissa nodded. "I want to be a singer. I dearly love to sing, and many women have mocked me for it. But when I came to Blessings, Ellie, the owner of the saloon overheard me singing and asked me if I would sing for her clients. I told her I wasn't that kind of woman, and I wouldn't disgrace my family in such a way. But she promised to help me put together a disguise, so no one would know it was me, and she also promised that the only thing I would do was sing. I wouldn't be forced to disgrace myself or participate in some of the improper activities that happen there."

The saloon. It was definitely not the place for a young lady of breeding, but Louisa could see that it would be the only place to sing around here.

"I understand better than you think. My sister and I were offered similar positions, only not as respectable. It's good that your respectability is being preserved, but I can see why you would want it to be secret and be a disguise."

"The women in my old town were unkind to me as well," Clarissa said. "But I didn't have the same optimism you had about my dream. You, at least, stand a chance. But what was there for me? I don't want to compromise my respectability, and yet I know that I endanger it every time I stand on that stage."

Louisa sat back down next to Clarissa. "Someday, we will live in a time when women are free to pursue whatever passions they choose. At least that is my hope. I will not judge you for your choice. It must be a terrible burden to have to carry."

Once again, she thought about Tom, and the burden her sister carried. How awful it must be for her to live life constantly pretending. As she looked over at Clarissa, she felt that same compassion.

"May I ask why you've told me all this?" Louisa asked gently. "Is there some way I can help?"

"As you might have gathered," Clarissa said. "I stay up late every night, because I'm at the saloon, singing. I've gone to great lengths to disguise myself and where I live, and so far, have not been discovered. But I'm so tired when I get home, I end up sleeping almost the entire morning. I find it difficult to function well before noon, and since my secret is no longer a secret from you, I was hoping that, rather than pretending I don't sleep so late, and feeling like you have to tiptoe around me when it comes to the children, could we come to an agreement?"

It seemed strange, bringing everything out into the open. At least now there was a reasonable explanation for Clarissa's behavior. And Louisa wouldn't need to feel so guilty about spending time with the children, worrying that someone would get in trouble.

"I would like that very much. As you may have guessed, they spend every morning here anyway. And, like you, this is an opportunity for me to live my dream in a way. I may not have an actual school, but I do give the children lessons every morning, and while it isn't the complete realization of my dream, it does fill a hole. I'm sure you aspire to more than singing in the saloon, but for now it satisfies, right?"

Clarissa smiled. "Exactly. I feel so guilty, sleeping in the morning, when I know I'm supposed to be caring for the children. But I don't, I'd have to give up the thing I dearly love most in the world. How does one choose?"

Louisa smiled back. "One doesn't. You ask for the support of your loved ones. I'm grateful you trusted me with your secret, and now I can help you."

She looked up at Jonah, who had given his sister another squeeze. "I am too. I never meant for this to be a way to keep you from living the life you dreamed of. I always assumed that your dream was like many women: that of a home and family. But I am even more happy to hear that it is your singing that inspires you."

He looked over at Louisa and smiled. "She has a magnificent singing voice. I didn't know why she stopped singing, and it made me sad. I didn't realize it was so she wouldn't be discovered by the saloon patrons. I'd still like to hear her sing, and maybe someday I can contrive a way to go listen to her one night."

Louisa looked up at him. "I could stay with the children one night."

The smile Jonah gave her warmed her. "You do not know how much that would mean to me. I am truly grateful for how much you have cared for my children, even if I haven't always been so gracious in showing it. I was in denial, not willing to accept that Clarissa wasn't doing a fine job with them. She used to be very good with them when I was home, and I didn't understand how things could have changed so drastically."

It seemed they had all misunderstood one another, and Louisa was grateful for the opportunity to clear everything up. She liked that about Jonah, that he was willing to talk things through and sort out any problems between them. Once again, she couldn't help thinking that he was a good man, one any woman would be proud to call husband.

No, she wouldn't allow herself to even think of it. A husband would ruin everything for her. And she wouldn't give up the love of her life, her first best, to be Jonah's second-best. He would never be able to love anyone the way he'd loved his first wife.

But seeing Jonah's loving acceptance of his sister's desires, and viewing women as being just as worthy of their dreams as any man, she felt a deep sadness in knowing that such a fine man as he was not available. At some point, she would like to know the kind of love her parents had for herself.

But she had to hope, that once she finished teaching, and she met a man, that God, in his infinite wisdom, would find her someone like Jonah or even better. She had to hold on to the hope that God wanted to give his children good gifts, and he would give her a better gift than the one she aspired to.

CHAPTER 9

*N*ow that the children had Clarissa's blessing to be at her house, things were different. The children had thought it fun to be at Louisa's when they were pulling a fast one on Clarissa. But now that everyone seemed united in the idea that the children should go over to Louisa's for lessons in the mornings, the children weren't happy with the arrangement. It had been easy enough for her to get them to do chores in exchange for another story or a new lesson, but now, as Louisa stared at the stubborn little girl who looked at her, arms crossed, in a battle of wills, she wondered what insanity had possessed her when she agreed to watch Jonah's children.

"I won't do it, and you can't make me," Callie said, staring her down.

"You're right. I can't. But Josephine has put her dog away and he won't come out until after you've done your chores. I know you were hoping to play with him, but there will be no playtime until your chores are done."

She looked down at the blank slate on the table. "You've

also not done your lessons. Both chores and lessons must be done in order to play."

If two children were this difficult to manage, how could Louisa have thought that becoming a schoolteacher would be easy? She didn't know what to do with them, not with such a drastic change. She glanced out the window, over at Jonah's house, hoping Clarissa would get up early today. Though that was unlikely.

Tom had been out late with the other miners, and they'd gone to see Clarissa's show. He said that Clarissa's voice was every bit as beautiful as others had said, perhaps even more so. One of the fellows Tom had been hanging out with had claimed to know their father. Tom had made it sound like their father had merely been a neighbor, and she was eager for news of an old friend. The man hadn't said much about it, but Tom was hoping that some time in the saloon might loosen his tongue.

But instead, her new acquaintance had found other entertainments, and some of the men were harassing Clarissa, so Tom spent the evening watching out for Clarissa instead.

"Louisa," Josephine called out from the yard. "Can you give me a hand lifting this?"

Louisa turned to the children. "You two behave yourselves and finish your lesson. I want to see the slates full of your letters, the words I gave you, and then we'll have a snack while I read to you."

Nathaniel groaned. "But I want a snack now. There weren't nearly enough eggs for breakfast today, and I'm still hungry."

It wasn't part of the arrangement that she feed the children breakfast, but she thought it a terrible crime that the only thing Clarissa ever left them was biscuits. She'd taken pity on the children and begun fixing them breakfast as well. But Josephine, ever stingy with her eggs, never gave them enough. Not that it was Josephine's problem. She was still hoping her prized hen would hatch something.

"Josephine and I went berry picking yesterday, and we found some delicious berries that we can eat as soon as you finish your lessons. The faster you work, the faster we can eat those berries."

The children made exasperated noises, but they bent down to their slates. Louisa went out to help her sister, and the wash tub was much fuller than it usually was. No wonder she'd needed help.

It took them several minutes to get the tub moved, but they did it. Funny how she used to look forward to the break from the backbreaking work, but now this was her respite. She and Josephine had already come up with a system for Louisa to tend the children while working on the laundry, so nothing had changed in her schedule, other than having Clarissa's blessing. But it felt different to her.

When she got back into the kitchen, the children sat at the table, strange expressions on their faces, and berry stains smeared across their mouths.

"I see you found yourself a snack," she said, trying not to laugh.

She and her sisters had picked strawberries, but these berries were ones she'd found on their excursion, perfect for Chel Santiago, a neighboring artist, who would crush them into powder and use them to make paints.

"They aren't delicious," Nathaniel said, looking cross.

"Hush. We didn't do anything," Callie said.

Louisa laughed. "The evidence is smeared all over your faces. And that is what you get for sneaking behind my back. Those berries aren't meant for eating, they're meant for making paint. Chel, one of our friends, uses them for her art. Had you been patient, you would have seen that the berries I meant to give you were strawberries."

She spied the bowl the children had taken. It still had a few berries left, so all was not lost, but it was disappointing that they'd have so little to give to Chel.

Josephine entered the room to get some more hot water from the stove. "What's going on here? Why are the children's face purple?"

"They thought that they were sneaking a treat, but instead, they got into the berries meant for Chel."

Josephine laughed. "Well that shows them, I guess. Based on what I've learned from the Miwok tribe, I don't believe they're poisonous, but I do understand they don't taste very good at all."

The children nodded in agreement.

"I shouldn't have tried to eat a whole handful at once," Nathaniel said.

Louisa glanced over at their slates, which were still empty.

"It's a terrible shame you didn't do your lessons as you were asked," she said. "I believe Josephine and I will share some of the berries and save the rest for your aunt and father. I'm sure they will appreciate them."

"What about us?" Callie asked.

Louisa shrugged. "Considering you tried to sneak all the berries and take them for yourselves, and you didn't do your lessons, I'm not sure you deserve any."

"But they were the wrong berries," Callie said, pounding on the table. "That's not fair."

Louisa went to the cupboard where she'd been keeping the berries in a bowl and took it out. She made a show of taking one of the berries and taking a bite. "Delicious."

But seeing the disappointment on the children's faces, Louisa couldn't help feeling a bit sympathetic toward them. After all, it wasn't often that they found fresh berries like these, particularly ones that were so tasty. They'd intended to put them all up for jam, but last night, waiting for Tom, she and Josephine had eaten far too many.

"I'll give you one more chance. But you absolutely must finish your lessons."

This time, the children bent to do their work, and Louisa was pleased with the progress. They worked diligently, and the work was as fine as they'd ever done.

Perhaps she had been hasty in thinking that the children were acting worse than usual.

Once the lessons were finished, she got out the bowl of strawberries and passed them around. It seemed, as they all ate, and Louisa read from her lesson book, they were back to where they'd once been. Even Callie's attitude toward her had softened, and she was back to her enthusiastic self.

Louisa's pleasure in the children's good behavior was short-lived. Only a few moments later, the children began arguing over who was taking up the most room on the bench. She let out a long sigh as she tried not to let it get to her. After all, they had been cooped up in the house doing lessons a lot longer than normal, thanks to their earlier misbehavior.

"Let's go outside and play a game, so we can have a little fun."

The children ran outside, and Louisa followed behind. Josephine had needed more hot water, so this was a good excuse to bring it to her. When she got outside, the children were running and playing as they normally did, and Louisa breathed a sigh of relief. Obviously, they'd just needed to stretch their legs a little. While she knew some people felt that children should be quiet and still all the time, she believed it went against their general nature.

Every child needed some time to have a little fun. After all, that's what adults needed, a bit of leisure to relax them and give them rest. Adult pastimes were quieter for the most part, but children should be allowed to be children. It wasn't a popular opinion in all circles, but it certainly was easier than trying to force children to be something they weren't.

Louisa dumped the water into the tub, and Josephine stood and stretched. "This is a rough batch," she said. "It's like the man rolled in mud."

The children let out a screech, as Callie shoved Nathaniel into a pile of manure. It might not have been mud, but it would have the same effect on the little boy's clothing. Tom had often remarked that she thought some of the men at the mine were nothing more than large children, so perhaps this is exactly what happened.

"Callie! You can't shove your brother like that," Louisa said, walking toward them.

"I can do what I want," she said.

Not this again. She went over to Nathaniel, who was crying. Louisa picked the little boy up and helped brush him off. "Are you all right? Are you hurting anywhere?"

Nathaniel shook his head. "She's just mad because I told her to put those berries away."

"What berries?"

He looked at his sister, who was hovering nearby. She could see the threat in the little girl's eyes.

"It's all right," Louisa said. "If Callie does anything to you, she'll be the one to get in trouble."

Nathaniel looked at the ground, then up at her. "The ones for the paints. Callie thought we should take them and make some of our own."

Callie glared at him. "You weren't supposed to tell. Now you've ruined it."

"But you didn't make paints. You broke your promise." Nathaniel's face scrunched up into a red mess of anger. "She threw them in there instead."

He pointed to the tub where Josephine had been soaking

another load of laundry. Louisa ran to the tub.

"What's wrong?" Josephine asked.

"Callie threw the berries we got for Araceli in here," Louisa said as she knocked over the tub. Hopefully they hadn't been in there long enough to do much damage.

As Josephine moved the clothing to a clean tub, Louisa turned to Callie.

"Why would you do such a thing?"

Callie glared at her. "I wanted to make you work more, to keep you too busy to tell us what to do."

Where had this horrible child come from?

Louisa turned to Josephine. "What's the damage?"

Her sister looked like she was about to cry. "Those were white. I was soaking them in a special solution to brighten them up for a lady staying at the hotel. But I think the dye in the berries will ruin everything."

"Let's see if we can undo the damage," Louisa said, taking one of the petticoats that was now tinged blue. Not a bright blue, so hopefully it was salvageable.

She scrubbed it with the special soap that she used to make things whiter, but it appeared to have no effect.

She turned and looked at Callie. "This is why you should never play tricks on anyone. We have a customer who is expecting her laundry, and now we're going to have to tell her that it was ruined."

As she spoke, Clarissa emerged from the house. "Good morning," Clarissa said, smiling.

It was almost miraculous, the change in the other woman's attitude toward her. They were almost like friends. Almost, but not quite, and Louisa feared telling her Callie's antics would ruin the friendship.

"Hello," Louisa said. "Callie, please tell your aunt what you just did."

Callie started to cry, but then she shook her head and ran

out of the yard and down the street.

"Callie!" Louisa started to chase after her, but she tripped on a rock and fell.

"What's this about?" Clarissa asked.

Josephine approached, wiping her hands on her apron, Nathaniel in tow. "Callie ruined a batch of laundry, thinking it would be a way to get out of lessons, but not realizing the damage it would do. I have a customer coming for them, and I don't know what I'm going to tell her."

She'd hung the evidence of Callie's crimes on the line, and Clarissa stared at it. "This is by far the worst thing she's ever done."

Louisa shook her head. "No, it's not. Running away now, that might be. It's not safe for her out there." She turned and bent in front of Nathaniel. "If your sister was upset, where would she go?"

Nathaniel shrugged. "Lots of places. Somewhere no one can find her."

"Please, Nathaniel. Tell us where she is. If you help us find her, I'll take you to the mercantile myself and you can pick out whichever piece of candy you want."

The little boy's eyes widened, but he shook his head. "I don't know. Besides, she won't like it if I tell."

Then he shrank back a little. "What are you going to do to me for not telling?"

Why were they all suddenly so afraid of her? She hadn't done anything to them. She didn't even raise her voice with them. And yet, both children acted like she was planning something terrible.

She knelt in front of him. "I'm not going to hurt either one of you. I want you both to be safe. That's the biggest reason why I'm worried about Callie running off like that. There are a lot of dangerous things in our town, and a child such as yourself, or your sister, could get really hurt.

Remember when you climbed the tree and fell and hurt your head? What happens if Callie tries to do something like that, and she's all by herself?"

Nathaniel rubbed his head. "I was all right though." Then he hesitated. "Do you really think Callie would get hurt?"

Louisa shrugged. "I don't know. But I'm afraid she would."

Clarissa let out a long sigh. "This isn't helping. He's obviously not going to tell. Trust me when I say I try all the time to get them to tell on each other. They have a deep loyalty to each other's secrets that can't be broken. We'd best go off in search of them on our own."

Josephine came from around the house. "She didn't go this way. But Clarissa is right. We should just go look for her."

"All right." Louisa took Nathaniel by the hand. "I'll take Nathaniel and we'll head out toward where Jonah is working. Maybe she has just gone to see her father."

Clarissa nodded. "And I'll take the other direction, that's the direction she ran in."

"I'll stay here, in case she comes back," Josephine said. "The town isn't very big, so she couldn't have gone far. But do check in from time to time with information about your progress. I can coordinate, and I'll make a note of where has already been searched so we don't duplicate efforts."

They all gave their agreement, and Louisa walked down the street with Nathaniel. She tried to take his hand, but he tugged away. "Nathaniel, why are you being so difficult? Have I done something to upset you? You used to always hold hands with me, and it's safer in the streets when we're holding hands."

Nathaniel kicked the dirt. "I don't need to hold your hand. We're not going to find Callie going this way. She would never go this way."

At least it was a start. But it still didn't explain the little boy's changed attitude toward her.

"Well, we'll at least go tell your father. He'll want to know your sister is missing, and perhaps even help us find her."

Nathaniel didn't say anything, but at least, this time, when she took his hand, he let her. As they rounded the corner to where Jonah was working, Louisa steeled herself for what she was going to say. What kind of schoolteacher, with only two charges, could lose one? Jonah had put so much faith in her, and she so easily let him down.

When they arrived at the building Jonah was working on, he spotted them immediately and walked over to them. "This is a nice surprise. What brings you here? And where is Callie?"

"She ran away" Nathaniel said, turning to glare at Louisa. "She ran away, and she's never coming back. Not so long as we have to stay with Louisa."

Jonah gave him a puzzled look. "What's wrong with Louisa?"

Nathaniel glared at her, then looked at his father. But he didn't say anything.

"I don't know what's gotten into them," Louisa said. "They've been inexplicably hostile to me these past few days, and I haven't a clue as to why. I keep trying to talk to them to figure out what's going on, but it doesn't seem to help."

Jonah shook his head. "I don't know either. But they've both been acting strange. I'll go look over at the Maguires. Their daughter, Isabella, is near in age to Callie."

Jonah indicated the direction they should go. "Let's see if Callie is there. If not, perhaps they will help us look for her."

Louisa reached for Nathaniel's hand, but he ran to his father. Jonah looked at her and shrugged, then took his son's hand.

It wasn't far, and when they got there, a woman stepped out of the house, wiping her hands on her apron. "Are you here for Callie? I don't mean to be rude, but while I'm happy to report that she's here safely, I do wonder at you letting her come all this way by herself. She told me you didn't mind, but I'll admit I was a little concerned."

Jonah straightened himself in the way he often did when faced with criticism of his children. "She did not have permission. In fact, she was being very disobedient by coming here without permission. I never let my children run around unattended, and they know that. Moreover, she was being given lessons by her schoolteacher at the time and I believe she ran away to avoid them."

The woman nodded slowly. "I was afraid of that. I do hope you didn't find me too critical. It's just not safe for a child her age to be wandering about on her own with all the riffraff about."

"I quite agree," Louisa said, smiling. "I'm Louisa Davidson, and I live next door to the Hastings family. I've also been teaching the Hastings children."

"Celia Maguire." A broad smile filled the woman's face. "I am delighted to make your acquaintance. A schoolteacher? In our little town? I was just telling Liam that it's a terrible shame that we haven't also thought about school for the children of Blessings. With new people moving in every day, some with families, it's a shame there's no safe place for the children. And, if Atherton Winslet truly wishes this to be a thriving community, then he must build a school to attract decent folk."

Then Celia looked around and gestured at the door. "But please do come in. Here I am yammering at you on the porch when we could be inside having a nice cup of tea."

Celia led them in to her cabin. It was a modest home, as they all were in Blessings, but she'd done her best to give her parlor a comfortable, settled feel.

"Girls. Callie's father is here. With the schoolteacher."

A screech, then a clatter followed from the other room. Louisa could hear Callie say, "Don't let her know I'm here. She'll take a switch to me for sure."

After a few more clatters, a little girl who looked to be about Callie's age, entered the room. "Callie isn't here. She's already gone home."

It was an awful lie, if Louisa had ever heard one. But Celia nodded. "That's a terrible shame," she said, raising her voice slightly. "I was going to open that can of cookies your Aunt Elsa sent me. I've been saving them for a special occasion, and having such fine company seems to be the perfect time to bring them out."

Taking the other woman's lead, Louisa spoke, also raising her voice slightly. "Oh, how delightful. What a wonderful treat for all of us. Perhaps, since Callie isn't here, Nathaniel can have her share."

Callie's desire to best her brother, or at least not be bested by him, won over her desire to hide. Callie raced into the room. "I haven't left yet. I was going to, but then I..." she looked around, wild-eyed. "I believe I lost my ribbon, and I was looking for it."

Jonah chuckled. "Is that so? Perhaps you should look on the end of your braid."

Callie looked down. "Oh. I see. Well, I guess I found my ribbon, and I'm here, so you needn't eat my cookie."

Celia nodded, smiling. "I'll just go put the kettle on. Isabella, please come help me."

The other woman looked at Louisa conspiratorially, like she understood what it meant to deal with a difficult child and was giving them time to remedy the situation.

"I'm very disappointed in you running away the way you did," Louisa said.

Jonah nodded. "And I as well. You know the rules. I understand that you've made a new friend, and naturally would want to spend time with her. But we must arrange these visits, and not impose on our new friends. Moreover, you can't just leave without telling someone where you've gone. But most importantly, you cannot be on the streets on your own. I don't know how many times I'm going to have to tell you that before you listen."

Callie lifted her chin. "I did what I thought I needed to do."She sounded so adult, and yet she was but a little girl, acting out.

"I don't care what you think you needed to do, there are rules and you must follow them," Jonah said.

Callie spun and turned her glare back on Louisa. "She was going to take a switch to me."

"I was going to do no such thing. How can you say that?"

Callie crossed her arms in front of her. "It's true. I did what was necessary to save myself."

Louisa turned and looked over at Jonah. "I can assure you, I have never taken a switch to her. Nor would I ever."

Jonah nodded slowly. "Why would you even say such a thing, Callie?"

"Because it's true. That's what schoolteachers do."

Louisa shook her head. "I've never met a schoolteacher who has. And I certainly wouldn't."

Celia entered the room, carrying a tray with tea and a plate attractively piled with cookies. "Well you know what they say, spare the rod and spoil the child. I'm sure if she was going to take a switch to you, she would have had good reason."

"But I wasn't," Louisa said. "Yes, you just ruined the clothing of a new customer, but my only intention was for you to confess what you'd done to Clarissa, so she could discuss it with your father, as well as the consequences."

Jonah looked over at her. "Is this true? She ruined some of your laundry?"

Louisa nodded. "I don't know what we're going to do. One of the women in the hotel had sent us her petticoats to be cleaned. She's only staying for a short time, and I can't imagine that they can be easily replaced. They looked very expensive. Josephine-"

Josephine. "Oh dear. I'd forgotten. Josephine was waiting at the house for news, and Clarissa had gone in the other direction in search of Callie. I do hate to cut this visit short, especially since you've gone to such great trouble with the refreshments. But I can't have them worry a minute longer."

Celia nodded. "Of course. I hadn't realized. You're absolutely right. But please, take some of these cookies with you. It would be a shame for them to go to waste, and it seems like you've had a terrible day and could use a treat."

"Thank you so much. Again, I am so sorry. But please, do call on me sometime so we might get to know one another."

Celia smiled. "That would be delightful. And you must come again. I would so appreciate the friendship of another woman."

"I would be pleased to do so," Louisa said, smiling. "Though I know Atherton has great dreams for Blessings, it's still a difficult place for women used to social activity."

"Indeed. And if you don't have your hands too full with Jonah's children, I would very much like to speak with you about teaching my children. I do what I can, but I would dearly love to have someone such as yourself working with them."

Considering the woman didn't even know her, it was high praise indeed. Perhaps even undeserved praise, considering she had just lost one of her charge.

So much for thinking her dream of being a schoolteacher could be so easily realized. Perhaps she was better off focusing on her family's laundry business and finding their father's killer.

CHAPTER 10

*A*s Louisa returned home, she said a prayer of thanksgiving that Callie had been found safely. But she spent the remainder of her walk asking the Lord for guidance about what she was supposed to do. She wasn't as helpful to Josephine because she had been spending so much time with Jonah's children. And though Josephine had said she didn't mind, Louisa often felt guilty for leaving her sister with most of the work. And then there was today's fiasco. What were they going to tell the customer?

As she entered her yard, she saw her question was about to be answered.

The customer, a Mrs. Agnes Goldsmith, of the St. Louis Goldsmiths, was pitching a fit in the middle of the yard.

"That was Italian lace. Irreplaceable. How could you be so foolish and clumsy?"

Louisa quickly joined her sister. "It was an unfortunate accident. I'm terribly sorry. Of course, we will pay for the replacement."

"Did you not hear what I told your sister?" The woman's voice raised, almost to a screech. "They are fine Italian lace.

You can't replace them. I would have to go to Italy again to purchase more. Are you going to finance my trip to Italy?"

Their lives would be easier if the woman was in Italy, but Louisa didn't need to count her share of the money she'd stashed away to know it wouldn't be nearly enough. As it was, it would be a number of years before they could afford a ranch of their own. But now, covering the damages the children had caused, it just might cost them everything.

Jonah approached, flanked by the man who had been waiting inside the carriage in front of the house when she'd arrived.

"What's going on?" Jonah asked.

"Agnes, darling. What has you in such a tizzy?" the man from the carriage asked.

Agnes's sobs continued as she turned to her husband. "These clumsy girls have ruined my petticoats."

"Just the other day, you were telling me how much you dislike them and wished for a new wardrobe."

The woman's sobs grew louder. "But you said no, and now I'm forced to wear this atrocity."

Agnes gestured at the now blue petticoats.

"Perhaps it will be considered fashionable," Jonah said.

Agnes spun to face him. "And who are you? You hardly look like an expert on fashion."

"I am not," Jonah said. "But surely we can work this out. I'm sure it was a terrible accident. The women typically do a wonderful job on the laundry. Everyone says that they're the best in town."

"Which is why I brought my laundry here," Agnes said. "But clearly everyone was mistaken, otherwise my laundry would not be ruined."

"As I've said," Louisa said. "I'm happy to compensate you for your loss."

Mr. Goldsmith nodded. "There, you see? They're willing

to make it right, and we'll be in San Francisco soon, where you can purchase new things."

At least the husband was being reasonable. Still, a lump formed in Louisa's throat as she thought about how much it would cost them. Fine Italian lace? She couldn't imagine the price they were going to put on them.

"How much do we owe you?" Josephine asked, her voice wavering.

"I'm sure I can't get anything new for less than fifty dollars," Agnes said.

Fifty dollars? Was the woman insane? They were petticoats, not ball gowns, and even then, Louisa couldn't see anyone paying such a ridiculous price.

But her husband nodded. "Yes, that sounds reasonable. I'm sure you can get some lovely replacements in San Francisco for that."

Louisa nodded slowly. "Yes, of course. I'll go get the money."

She went into the house and dug into the place Tom had built for them to keep their valuables under the floorboards. Fifty dollars. Nearly the entirety of their savings.

She took the money and brought it out to them, noting the way Agnes's nose crumpled as she counted the bills. "Such filthy money. I can't imagine being forced to carry this around."

Filthy money? Money was money, no one cared whether or not it was dirty.

But her husband patted her arm. "Don't worry, my pet. We'll change it out at the bank."

These people were extraordinary. And not in a good way. She pointed at the petticoats. "They're not quite dry, but we could fold them up for you."

Agnes shook her head. "I would not be caught dead with something so disgraceful. I can't even give them to my maids to wear. It would be scandalous. Keep them. Burn them for all I care, because that's all they're good for now."

Blue or not, they were still serviceable, and worn under enough layers, most people wouldn't even know. But Louisa wasn't going to argue with the woman. Better to get rid of her now.

Once the Goldsmiths left, Jonah shook his head. "Those people are unbelievable. Fifty dollars for petticoats? Why would you pay such a price?"

She turned to face him. "Because this is my livelihood. Our family depends on our income from our laundry, and they were right to be angry at how hers was ruined. Imagine if on one of your jobs, you sawed through someone's beautiful mantle that had been hand carved in Italy. What would you do?"

He nodded slowly. "I hadn't thought of that. But still, how could such a thing have happened?"

She'd been hoping the children would tell him more than what he'd learned at the Maguires'. That was how they got into this whole mess. Because she'd wanted Callie to admit to her aunt what she'd done. But that had only made Callie run away and tell everyone Louisa was going to take a switch to her. So fine then. She'd tell him.

"Callie decided to play a trick on me, to keep me so busy, she wouldn't have to do any work. She tossed some berries meant for paints into the wash tub. Unfortunately, it contained these lovely, apparently priceless, petticoats. The dye in the berries ruined them."

Jonah stared at her. "I'm sure it was an accident. Callie wouldn't do such a thing intentionally."

Louisa stared at him. "She admitted she did it intentionally. I know she didn't know that would ruin the laundry, but it did. She ran away because I was trying to get her to tell Clarissa what she'd done."

The children had come upon them as she was speaking. Louisa turned and looked at Callie. "Now tell him. Tell him what you did today."

Callie shook her head. "I didn't do anything. She's making it up."

Jonah looked at his daughter, then back at Louisa. "Why would Callie lie?"

"She's obviously afraid of getting in trouble. You heard her at the Maguire house. She was afraid I was going to take a switch to her, even though I assured her I've never done such a thing, and I never will."

He looked over at Callie. "Why would Louisa tell such a story about you?"

Callie shrugged. "Because she's mean. You don't know her. She's mean."

"Callie, I must insist on knowing why you persist in telling people that I'm being mean to you. I pride myself on being kind to every living being, and I would certainly never be unkind to someone I have grown to love so much. Please tell me specifically what I have done that is mean, not only so that I may defend myself, but also, so that if there is a defect in my character, that I may improve upon it."

Her words weren't entirely for the little girl, but for the man staring suspiciously at her. How could he say, after all of the conversations they'd had, that she would ever do anything to hurt his children? And why would he give so much weight to their word over hers?

Callie started to cry. "You just are. And you're being mean to me again."

Louisa knelt in front of the little girl. "If holding you accountable for your actions is what you mean by being mean, then yes, I am. We must all accept responsibility for ourselves and our actions, even when it's difficult. I know you didn't intend to cause so much damage, but you must understand that all of our actions have consequences, and you need to own up to what you've done."

Callie turned and fled into her house. Louisa stood to look at Jonah. "I'm sorry for upsetting her, and for causing disruption in your family. But you don't know the full story, so you cannot appreciate how difficult the situation is for me."

He nodded slowly. "You're right, I don't. I have yet to hear my daughter's side of things. I'm very troubled that she's afraid to speak of it."

Jonah almost sounded like he thought Louisa was at fault. But surely she misunderstood.

"You're right," Louisa said. "We haven't heard from Callie. And I've been trying all day to get her to open up to me. Perhaps you will have better luck."

She looked back over her shoulder at her sister, who had picked up one of her chickens and was sitting on a stump with her back to them. Knowing Josephine, she was probably sobbing quietly, and telling her chicken how terrible it was that their plans for the future would be delayed.

All of this was Louisa's fault. For wanting to be a school teacher. For thinking that she could take a shortcut to her dreams while ignoring those of her family. She hadn't done much to help her sisters lately, being so consumed with teaching Jonah's children. And now, because of Jonah's children, it had cost them fifty dollars of their savings.

All thanks to Louisa and her crazy idea that she could be a school teacher.

She squared her shoulders as she looked Jonah in the eye. "I'm terribly sorry to have to do this to you, but I don't think my caring for your children is working out. I have been neglecting our laundry business, and today's incident, though it was an accident, proves that I cannot have my attention divided. My sister needs me, and I must put my family before yours. I hope you will find a solution to your family's situation soon."

She turned and started to walk away, but Jonah called out after her. "Wait."

Louisa turned. "I won't change my mind."

"I'm not asking you to. I don't know what happened today with my children, but until today I have never heard Callie saying anything about someone taking a switch to another person. That's not how I raise my family. You say you've never threatened to do something, but her fear is very real, so I have to believe that she got the idea from somewhere."

Her stomach hurt at his words. Was this what life as a teacher was like? Being accused and then blamed without evidence? She'd done nothing wrong, at least as far as she knew.

"I can't say that I agree with you, because as I have said numerous times, I have never made such a threat. But you don't believe me, and I accept that. I would appreciate it if your children did not come over here again."

She hated adding that last part, but she didn't know what else to say. They'd gotten into this mess in the first place because Jonah's children came over without permission. And now she knew better. She'd done what she thought was a kindness, only to be hurt in the end.

That might not have been what Jonah intended, but he'd too readily accepted his daughter's story without looking into the matter on a deeper level. She could understand that he loved her and wanted to believe the best of her. And even Louisa didn't believe the little girl's actions were from a place of malice. But clearly, he wasn't willing to communicate with her, and where she once felt twinges of something at his smile, she only felt sadness.

The fickleness of romantic feelings was exactly why she hadn't found love for herself. Why would she give up her dream for something like that? As Jonah left, Louisa walked to her sister's side, where she could hear Josephine's quiet sobbing.

Louisa sat next to her and put her arm around her. "I'm sorry," she said. "I was selfish in my belief that I could be a teacher without giving a thought to how it impacted the rest of the family. I've placed a lot of the burden on your shoulders these past few weeks, and I'm sorry. I'll do a better job in the future, I promise."

Josephine turned and put her head on Louisa's shoulder, shifting the chicken in her arms as she did so. "I'm not just crying for me. I'm crying for you. How could Jonah be so blind? There were a few times when I thought he might even be falling in love with you, but it was an illusion. And so, it leaves me to wonder if love is really possible. I know it's silly of me, but I always thought that someday, I could meet a man who loved me as much as I love my animals. If you, who are not nearly so odd as I, cannot find love, what hope is there for me?

Her sister's words burned a hole in her heart. She'd known, of course, that Jonah could never love her because he loved his late wife too much. But she hadn't thought that others would be watching and learning from their example. "I knew he did not love me. But I did think he liked me. And I did hope we were friends. But that betrayal doesn't hurt so much as the fact that it cost us so much of our hard-earned savings, money we would have used for a ranch."

Josephine looked up at her and wiped the tears from her eyes. "It's a setback, but that is a dream I know we can make happen. It's something tangible and real. And with you helping me, and all your attention on our business, we can do it."

Even though the day's loss had been absolutely devastating in terms of their income, Louisa's dreams, and what she thought were friendships, she appreciated the newfound strength it gave her.

Josephine was right. So many things she hoped for in her life were intangible, and there was no way of knowing she could ever get them. But the ranch, that was something they could strive for.

CLARISSA HAD TAKEN him to task over not getting the full story from Louisa. In part, Jonah knew she was right. However, he wasn't sure he knew what to trust. After Clarissa's revelations about Lily, he'd mentally gone back through his life with her, trying to see how he had missed all the signs that Lily was unkind to his sister. And he still didn't know.

Which was why, the next morning, instead of getting up early to go to work as he always did, he went out and started to build a fence between the two properties. Maybe he didn't have answers, but he could at least keep his children from going over there and keep his end of the bargain with Louisa.

After he drove the first post in, he pulled his hat off and wiped his brow. Atherton Winslet was approaching, and Jonah tried not to groan. At the barn dance the other night, the older man had nudged him and told him he should ask Louisa to dance. He'd refused, saying his heart was fully in the grave, but the older man had chuckled and told him that God had other plans sometimes.

Whatever that meant.

And now he was here to witness him building a fence between the two properties, a sign for certain Jonah and Louisa would never be together.

"What's that you're building?" Atherton gave him a broad smile, but Jonah wasn't fooled.

"A fence. My children have been disturbing the Davidson

sisters at work, and apparently because of it, a load of laundry was ruined yesterday."

Callie refused to talk about it, and instead cried when he'd asked her about it. He'd never seen his daughter so upset, not even when her mother had died. Something terrible must have happened for Callie to be so upset, and he hoped, that by giving her time, she would feel more comfortable telling him.

Atherton nodded. "Ah, yes. Mrs. Goldsmith's famed petticoats. We had to listen to her tell the tale over dinner, of how she got the petticoats and of how the inconsiderate laundress I recommended ruined them. I was coming by to be sure that the only person upset about the situation is Mrs. Goldsmith. Mr. Goldsmith is quite pleased with himself because he got fifty dollars out of the deal, and the man does love his money."

Jonah nodded. "She said they were very expensive."

"Quite. The best Italian lace money can buy. I wonder how those girls were able to afford the fifty dollars they gave the family."

Jonah hadn't thought about it. But at Atherton's intense stare, he wished he had.

"Accident or not, if your children were somehow involved, especially given that you're now building a fence as a result, you might consider repaying the girls for what they spent."

He stared at the older man. Atherton was asking him to give the Davidson sisters the money? But just as quickly as indignation rose in him, he let out a long sigh. Regardless of who was at fault, his children had been involved. And he'd been too stubborn to get the full story from Louisa.

"I don't know what happened," Jonah said. "Callie won't tell me, and Louisa is angry with me."

Atherton kicked at the fence post. "Angry enough for a

fence? That's some anger. But I would be angry too, if I came to town for a fresh start, and my neighbor's troublesome children cost me fifty dollars. Especially since that fifty dollars was going to go toward a ranch that would get me the home I'd always dreamed of, and away from said pesky neighbor. Maybe what those girls need more than a fence, is the fifty dollars back."

He couldn't accuse the older man of being subtle, and the way Atherton was looking at him, he knew that wasn't his goal.

Jonah nodded. "In theory, yes. But Louisa was supposed to be watching them. We'd come to an agreement. Since it was done on her watch, shouldn't she be at fault for not watching them properly?"

"Perhaps you don't know the whole of the story. Which is why you should talk to her and listen to what she has to say."

Jonah glanced over at the Davidson house, where the sisters were already busying themselves with work.

"I could, but even if I gave her fifty dollars, it wouldn't change things between us."

"Maybe not, but it would go a lot further than the fence you're building."

"Who says I have fifty dollars to spare?"

Atherton looked him up and down, then back over at the girls. "And who says they did? They've only begun saving for the ranch, and I know, with the work I've sent you, you've probably got quite a bit stashed away to buy the property they're now on. But I suppose, if your dream is more important than their dream, then you aren't the man I thought you were."

Before Jonah could respond, Atherton continued toward the women. He felt sick, being called out like that, but Atherton was right. He did have the fifty dollars. He was so close to having the funds to buy that land, and though fifty dollars would come again, he hated the thought of taking that much longer.

But what would he do? Buy the land, then throw the girls out before they were ready? He wasn't that horrible of a person. But obviously, he was horrible enough that he'd let Louisa pay for the entirety of a mistake that was at least partially Callie's.

He turned back into the house, and found Callie sitting at the table, happily munching on a biscuit with jam. "Good morning Papa. It's nice to have you here."

She smiled at him, and he knew that the children didn't like how much he worked. But he wanted to work while it was plentiful, while he had the ability to do so. Slow times were coming, as they always did, especially come winter.

And if it wasn't for what happened between Callie and Louisa yesterday, Jonah would be at work. He'd told Clarissa to sleep today and he would manage for the morning. He wouldn't be up to doing this forever, but for now, it seemed to be the easier way.

"It's just until I can find someone else to care for you. Which is why I want to know what happened with Louisa. I want to be sure it doesn't happen again."

Callie dropped the biscuit on the table. "I told you. She was going to take a switch to me."

"But why? What happened with the laundry?"

Nathaniel stumbled into the room, rubbing his eyes. "Papa. What are you doing home?"

"I'm building a fence between our house and Louisa's. Since you two can't stop bothering them, I have to come up with a better solution. Whatever the two of you did yesterday, it cost them a great deal of money."

Nathaniel ran to him. "Please don't build a fence. I want to be able to go to see Miss Louisa. I didn't do it. Callie did.

She was mad at Miss Louisa for making us do our lessons, so she said she was going to play a trick on her."

Which meant it wasn't an accident. Probably the ruining of the laundry was, because Callie couldn't have possibly known the damage those berries would do. But she had meant to hurt Louisa, and it made Jonah feel sick inside.

He turned his attention to Callie. "Why would you do such a thing? Louisa has been nothing but kind to you."

Callie scowled. "That was before she was my schoolteacher. Everyone knows that schoolteachers are mean. Isabella told me she was glad to have moved here because now she doesn't have to go to school with that nasty schoolteacher Miss Prosser."

All this over a fear? "So Louisa hasn't done anything to you. You just feared she might, because you heard that's what schoolteachers do, is that right?"

Callie nodded. "Isabella says her schoolteacher took a switch to her. And her mother said she was right to do so."

After Celia's comment about sparing the rod and spoiling the child, he could understand. But Louisa was different. And not only had she never done any such thing, as she'd claimed, the more he thought about it, the more he realized that she was completely incapable of it.

"Did Louisa actually threaten to take a switch to you, or did you just fear she would?"

Callie shook her head.

But rather than making him feel better about the situation and going to Louisa with an apology and the money he clearly owed her, it only made him feel worse.

Clarissa stepped out of her room, yawning.

"I told you I would take care of the children today. Go back to bed. You need your sleep."

Clarissa shook her head. "It was a slow night. That Goldsmith fellow from yesterday came in with some other gentleman. They were quite unruly and demanded that I do more than sing. It got uncomfortable, but that fellow from next door, Tom, was there again, and he helped me get away. He didn't know who I was, and I felt guilty for not telling him. He's a good man, and his actions reminded me that Louisa is a good person. We've maligned her so much since they've moved in, and like Tom rescued me from those men, I believe that she only wants to help others."

Clarissa walked over to where Callie was seated at the table. "Jam? Where did you find that?"

Callie smiled. "I just did, that's all."

Clarissa turned and ran to her room, but within a few moments had returned.

"That was the last jar of jam. You stole it from my room."

Then Clarissa shrugged. "Well then. At least now you know what it's like to have no jam. I was saving that for your birthday, because I know how much you love jam. So, this year, there will be no treats for your birthday. I hope you're satisfied."

Clarissa turned to Jonah. "I know you love your children and want to believe the best of them. But Callie is very good at telling tales, and she walks around like she owns the world. She'd have had to go through my things, my private things, to get to the jam. It wasn't like what you discovered in my room."

"I knew there was more jam," Callie said calmly. "You were being selfish and not sharing it with us."

Jonah shook his head. "She'd just gotten done telling you that it was to be for your birthday."

The unrepentant expression on his daughter's face made Jonah sick. He'd blindly believed in her, blindly believed in Lily. He took the biscuit out of her hand. "Where did you put the rest of the jam?"

Callie shrugged. How had he raised such an insolent

child? He hardly recognized the sweet little girl that he loved. No wonder Louisa had said she was being difficult. He'd thought she was exaggerating, but this was a side of Callie he hadn't seen before. Perhaps he had been spending too much time working and not enough time paying attention to his children except for when they were on their best behavior.

"Tell me where the jam is."

Callie stared at him. "You can't take my biscuit. That's mine."

"But you took it from your aunt. It was hers."

Callie glared at him. "If my mother was alive, this wouldn't have happened. If it wasn't for you ruining her figure by forcing her to have another baby, she would still be here. And I wouldn't have to deal with Aunt Clarissa or Louisa. Mama let me do whatever I wanted. She said I was pretty and clever, just like her."

He had been blind. The things that came out of his daughter's mouth were not things he'd heard before, but from the expression on Clarissa's face, she wasn't surprised. He'd clearly been trying too hard to make a living for his family to understand what was happening in his life.

"I'm sorry your mother said those things to you. She never said them to me."

Callie gave him a look that was wise beyond her years. "Why would she? Mama always said that we just have to be cute and sweet and you would give us whatever we wanted. And it's worked."

A dark expression filled her face. "Until now."

Jonah nodded. "You are correct. Things are going to change around here, and one of them is that you are going to give everyone your absolute respect. And no more of these games."

He looked over at Nathaniel. "Have you had breakfast yet?"

The little boy shook his head. Jonah handed him Callie's biscuit. "Take this. It may be the last we get of jam for quite some time."

Nathaniel smiled. "She always hogs it for herself. If there's any left, it's in Mama's trunk by her bed."

Callie jumped out of her seat. "How dare you tell on me."

Nathaniel shrugged. "You haven't been very nice since you met Isabella."

He turned and looked at his father. "Isabella isn't very nice. At the barn dance, she and Callie were playing mean games. They were playing tricks on everyone."

He looked down at the ground. "They dumped water on me and told everyone I wet my pants."

Clearly, while some of this was definitely her mother's influence, some of it had also been her new friend.

Jonah held his arms out to his son. "Thank you for telling me. I wish you'd told me when it happened. It was wrong of your sister to make you wet your pants and to play tricks on people. Tricks are not very fun, and they cost people a lot."

He thought to the fifty dollars he owed Louisa. "Callie, your prank on Louisa cost her fifty dollars yesterday. I'm going to give her back the money on your behalf and you are going to repay me. I will find tasks for you to do in addition to your regular chores. I will keep track in my ledger, and I imagine it will be quite some time before you repay me. But you will repay me. And you will apologize to Louisa."

Callie looked at the ground. "We were just having fun."

If his daughter hadn't learned much about kindness from her mother, how could he expect her to understand?

For the first time, Callie looked truly sorry for what she'd done. But it made him sad to see how much it had taken to get her to that point. So many things he hadn't noticed or caught on to, and now he was at a loss, wondering what was the truth, and what was a lie.

Lily hadn't always gotten along with the women in their acquaintance. She'd always said it was because they were jealous, and Jonah had left it at that. But as he thought about all the times he'd thought he'd walked in on something, only to be dismissed by Lily, he realized he had been blinded by his love for her. Just like with Callie's misbehavior. He couldn't have imagined that she would be so ill behaved, and now, he would have to do a lot of work to change that.

Clarissa smiled at him, reminding him of another situation where he'd been blinded to the truth, but once it was revealed, everything had worked itself out.

He looked out the window and noticed that Atherton had left. He didn't want the older man to read too much into the situation. He didn't seem to understand that Jonah and Louisa were firmly off the market.

Especially now.

If he'd learned anything since the Davidson sisters had arrived, it was that he couldn't trust himself when it came to those he loved. How was he to judge correctly and see the truth? He didn't want to be in that situation again, particularly because his blindness kept hurting people. Worse, he'd done a disservice to his loved ones because of it. How was he supposed to know and judge correctly when it came to people in his heart?

He turned to Clarissa. "I'm going to go talk to her. I've done her a grave disservice and I don't know how to make things right."

Clarissa reached out and gave him a hug. "As you recall, it wasn't too many days ago that I had to do the same thing. Like you, I was fearful of Louisa's reaction, but the thing I have truly come to appreciate about her is her compassion and grace for others. Give her a chance."

It sounded so easy, yet the thought was terrifying. He could relate to how Clarissa had felt. Well, if he could make her do it, he could do it, too. He grabbed the money from its hiding spot to take to her. When he went outside, he got no farther than the fence line he'd started to build, and he felt sick. Really and truly sick. If one could die of mortification, he would.

But before he could cross that line, Tom approached. "I heard about what happened."

Jonah nodded. "And I am terribly sorry about it. How wrong I was. I did Louisa a great disservice by not talking to her and letting her share her side of the story. I didn't even give her a chance, and I was wrong."

Tom nodded slowly. "Yes, you were. I've never seen my sister so unhappy, and that's saying something, considering the last time she was unhappy was when she found out that the Board of Education gave the teaching job she was promised to a male cousin of theirs, even though he had a less than savory character. Better for them to hire an unsavory man than her, at least that's how she saw it. It hurt that none of her friends stood behind her."

If he'd been the kind of friend he'd claimed to be, he would have stood behind her as well. Yesterday.

"I'm hoping to make amends."

Tom gestured at the fence he'd started building. "By building a fence?"

Jonah sighed. "It wasn't one of my better ideas. When I'm upset, or I have a problem I'm trying to work out, I build things."

Tom nodded. "Josephine was wanting a better fence so that she could let her chickens roam little more freely, so it will be welcome."

"And Louisa?"

Tom shrugged. "Man-to-man, I'm asking you to leave my sister be. I'm sure you mean well by coming to apologize to her, and I do believe you owe her one. But she needs time first."

Jonah let the other man's words sink in. Tom was barely a man, little more than a boy. But Jonah appreciated the way he stood up for his sister. Jonah would've liked to have thought he'd have done the same for his, but he'd missed the fact that his wife had been mistreating her.

Jonah nodded. "All right then." He reached into his pocket and pulled out the money he'd taken from the box he was using to save up.

"Could you give her this? It's fifty dollars to cover what she paid for the ruined petticoats. If they lose more business because of my daughter's actions, I'm willing to compensate them for that, too. It isn't right that your family should suffer for my family's actions."

Tom took the money and stared down at it. "Fifty dollars."

Then he looked up at Jonah and laughed. "Can you imagine spending fifty dollars on petticoats? I consider it a great blessing that my sisters aren't so frivolous."

The other man's attempt at humor made Jonah smile. Fifty dollars was ridiculous to pay for petticoats, and he pitied poor Mr. Goldsmith for having such a wife. But he was also grateful that Tom was attempting to normalize things between them.

Perhaps someday he would get the chance to speak with Louisa to make things right.

CHAPTER 11

he children were outside playing again. Even though they were on the other side of the fence, and she couldn't see them, she could still hear them, and they sounded happy. Not that she wished them ill, because she didn't, but because it created a deeper longing in her than she would have expected. She'd been missing them terribly.

And not just them, but their father. It was odd, missing him, considering she could hear him outside almost every day, playing with his children. He wasn't very far, just a few footsteps, but given everything that had happened between them, it felt like miles.

After he had come to try to apologize, Tom had returned with the money, telling her what Jonah had said. It was a kind gesture, giving them the money, and even though Louisa had been upset over losing the money, it really wasn't about that at all. She'd been hurt, and even though Jonah had said he'd wanted to apologize, it didn't seem like he tried very hard. Maybe it was unfair of her to want an apology in her way, but she didn't know what else to do.

She'd been too hurt over everything. And now, she wasn't

sure how to move forward. Especially since she wasn't sure what was left for her. Yes, an apology would be good, but what point would it serve? Being hurt by Jonah had only pointed out to her how deeply her feelings were entangled with his. She didn't want to rely on a man, fall in love with him, and have to give up everything she wanted.

Besides, this wasn't just about her dreams, but her sisters'. She'd let her desire to be a teacher, even in a small capacity, get in the way of her family's greater dream, of bringing their father's murderer to justice, and building a new ranch for their family.

Even though people had heard about Mrs. Goldsmith's petticoats, they'd only lost a few clients. And those they'd lost were replaced by new clients, some of which wanted to come to see the petticoats. Atherton had visited them next day, wanting to see the petticoats as well. It was amazing to see the ruckus a few blue petticoats could cause. Louisa couldn't help thinking of Joseph and his brothers and how what had been intended to harm Joseph, God had used for good.

Josephine materialized behind her. "I think you got the stain out of that shirt five minutes ago."

Louisa looked up at her and sighed. "I'm sorry. You're right."

Josephine smiled. "Don't be too hard on yourself. I know you miss them. I've wondered, why haven't you gone to speak to them? Tom said Jonah wanted to apologize, and I know he sent around a note. You haven't even opened it."

Louisa sighed as she wrung out the shirt and held it up to the light. "You're right, the stain is gone. If only things were so simple with Jonah."

Louisa gave a small shrug. "Jonah didn't just hurt my pride, but my heart. I know it's foolish of me to have feelings for him, but I've always held him in high regard. I never imagined we could be together, because he's always been so deeply in love with his late wife. But after he cut me so deeply, I realized that deep down, I wished he could love me like that."

She sighed and reached for another shirt. "But the fact is he can't. He won't. And even though we all said we would marry for love, it doesn't feel much like love when only one person feels that way. And what is wrong with me, thinking myself in love with a man who can't return my feelings? My heart isn't safe with him. And I can't bear to read an apology, which I'm sure that letter contains, when the last thing I need is to feel warm feelings for him again. My heart can't take it. It isn't fair to me."

Josephine nodded. "Are you sure there's no chance he could love you? I've seen how he looks at you."

Louisa shook her head. "Even you can't be so naive as to think that when a man looks at a woman a certain way, it's about love."

Josephine chuckled. "True. I feel sorry for Tom. One of the miners she thinks might have known our father keeps inviting him to the saloon. She's confessed to me that it's dreadfully embarrassing being around all those people carrying on the way they do."

Louisa sighed. "Do you think Tom will ever find love? I fear what Edward did to her will make her think she cannot be loved. But I know there's a man out there for her."

She began washing another shirt and she smiled up at her sister. "Just as I believe there is love for both of us. I don't know how, or where. But it's somewhere."

Josephine pointed at the house. "Go inside and read Jonah's apology. Maybe it's where you'll find love for yourself."

Louisa shook her head. "Being fanciful hurt our family. And even though we did get the money back, and our business hasn't suffered, I'm afraid of Jonah hurting me again.

And what happens if I marry? We've already decided that Tom must go somewhere else to regain her identity. How can I ask that of a husband and children?"

The crunch of boots on gravel made her turn. Tom.

"Then I'll remain as I am. I hear the way men joke about women who aren't perfect in their eyes. No one will settle for someone less than that. And so long as you both are unmarried, I must remain a man to protect you. But, I think Josephine is correct. Jonah did seem sincere in his apology. And as for his feelings, neither one of you have discussed it with each other. Maybe you tell him how you feel and see how he responds."

"A woman doesn't declare herself to a man. Besides, I don't know that I've forgiven him."

Then she shrugged. "Well, technically, I have. I know he was acting in the best interest of his family. But what happens next time? You can forgive someone, but that doesn't mean you need to let them hurt you again. I don't know if I'm ready to let Jonah hurt me again."

She thought back to what Tom had said about remaining a man. She turned to face her sister. "And it's not fair to ask you to stay a man forever."

Tom shrugged. "Even though the men joke around about me being not quite a man, or more boy than man, they treat me with far more respect than anyone ever did when I was a woman. I miss my dresses, and I miss all the things we used to do together as women. But, for the first time in my life, I can walk through town with my head held up high, without worrying about how people are going to receive me, and without women laughing behind their fans at me. I'm not sure I'm willing to give that up."

Louisa stared at her. "But what about marriage and a family?"

Tom sighed. "I don't have an answer for that. I would very much like children someday, but what man will accept me?"

She put her hands to her beard and let out another long sigh.

Louisa wished she could argue with her sister, but she'd witnessed the taunts. It made her sad to know that Tom wasn't able to live freely as herself.

Josephine walked over to where Louisa was standing and put her arm around her. "I think what we're both saying, is that if you love him, and you want to make a life with him, then do it. Don't worry about putting us out or hurting us. We'll manage. And even though I know the two of you are set on finding father's murderer, let's be honest. After two months, we've come no closer to finding the truth than we were when we first got here."

"That's not exactly true," Tom said. "I found a man who had drinks with him."

Louisa let out a long sigh. "And George Washington. That man's crazy as a loon, so to take his word about our father, it seems silly."

Josephine set her chicken down. "Remember that rancher I told you about, Miguel? His ranch was nearly forty miles from ours. Not close enough to know anything about Father, but the same bank that had the mortgage on his place had the mortgage on ours."

"Don't you find that suspicious?" Louisa asked. "That the same bank would hold mortgages on ranches forty miles apart? I thought our bank was too small for such things."

"They didn't have our mortgage at all. It was some outfit out of San Francisco," Tom said. "That's the part I find suspicious. Why didn't father use our local bank? Why would he go all the way to San Francisco for a loan? And why would our banker, Mr. Cavins, a man we have known our entire lives, refuse to lend us the money to pay off the mortgage when he knew we'd helped Father run the ranch all these years and could eventually pay him back?"

Josephine groaned. "We've been through this. It's because we're women. No one wants to give a woman a mortgage. We know that. We should just move on with our lives, save up the money we need for a ranch, and build one."

Once again, Louisa felt torn between her two sisters. On one hand, Josephine was right. Yes, it was odd that their father would get a loan on the ranch from some bank in San Francisco. It was also strange that the same bank would lend money to another ranch forty miles in another direction. But that was the only thing they could find about their father's death. Obviously, Atherton Winslet didn't kill him. And, the blacksmith was too drunk to tell them anything. They were completely out of clues, and out of hope.

But, as Louisa saw the pain on Tom's face, she knew they couldn't give up. Tom had been especially close to their father, and to see her so sad, it made Louisa want to continue with their quest. It wouldn't bring their father back, but if it could give Tom some peace of mind, she would do that for her sister.

"Enough about all this. Louisa, go read the letter." Tom gave her a shove in the direction of the house, where the letter had been sitting on the kitchen table since Jonah had brought it over a week ago.

She went inside and made herself a cup of tea for fortification, and then, she slipped the envelope open.

DEAR LOUISA,

I am greatly troubled by the pain I have caused you. It must be a deep wound indeed for you to refuse to speak to me. I am hoping that by sending you a letter, you will at least read it, and not toss it into the fire.

I cannot begin to express how sorry I am for not hearing you out. You were right, and since that day, I have spent a great deal of time with my children, learning about them, and realizing that I didn't know them as well as I thought I did. I've come to realize that when I love someone, I am blinded to their faults. And I'm sorry that my blindness has caused you pain.

I would also be remiss if I didn't tell you that the children miss you as well. I do not believe Callie realized the magnitude of her actions, which were based out of fear planted in her by a new friend. We've since spoken both to her and her friend about this fear, and she is extremely distraught at pushing away someone who loved her so dearly.

I'm not asking you to resume your position with us, because I realize there is much to repair in a relationship before then, but I would like for you to consider at least allowing us back into your life. You have become a dear and valuable friend to us, and we have used you most poorly. I pray you will forgive me, forgive us, because there is a hole in our lives without you.

I am enclosing letters from the children as well. Sincerely, Jonah Hastings

SHE TURNED the page and found a note from Nathaniel.

DEAR MISS LOUISA, I'm sorry. Please play games with me again.
Love Nathaniel

THE SPELLING WAS WRONG, and since the child was not used to using a pen, the letters were splotchy, but she could tell he had been practicing. And that he had written it himself. Her heart warmed as she realized that she had done some good.

Even in their short time together, she had taught the boy something.

She flipped the page to a letter from Callie.

Dear Miss Louisa,

I'm sorry for the trick I played. It was wrong. I miss spending time with you. I promise I will never play another trick on you again. Please come back. Love, Callie

WHEN SHE FLIPPED that page over, her eyes were full of tears. They'd missed her just as much as she missed them. But it didn't mean her heart could take coming back.

As Louisa wiped the tears from her eyes, a knock sounded at the door.

She opened it to find Atherton standing there.

"I was hoping to have a word with you."

As she let him in, she took a deep breath to regain her composure.

"With all the new families moving into Blessings, we've had a great deal of interest in starting a school."

She nodded slowly. Celia had been by a couple of times, and each time she'd dropped some not-so-subtle hints that she would dearly love for Louisa to work with her children. However, she told the other woman no, because she needed to help her sister with their laundry business.

"I've donated a piece of land, and I talked to the people at the lumberyard and they're willing to donate the lumber. Jonah Hastings has agreed to donate his carpentry skills and a number of the other men have agreed to help him. It's going to be a good old-fashioned barn raising, and everyone is going to contribute. I've talked to the community, and we all agree that you would be the perfect person to become the town's schoolteacher."

He smiled at her like he was doing her a big favor, and had the offer come a couple months ago, she would have jumped at the chance. But now she hesitated.

Atherton continued. "Now, don't think that we're going to take advantage of your good nature and impose upon you. You'll be paid, just like with any other schoolteacher position. Most towns the families take turns boarding the schoolteacher. But since you have a home here, I've asked each family to contribute to a fund that would pay you a decent salary."

He named a wage that was more than fair. It was higher than what she would have been making had she gotten the position in their old town.

But as she looked out the window, to see her sisters standing there, eagerly waiting to see what business Atherton had for her, she shook her head. "It's a fine offer, and I would gratefully accept. However, I cannot leave my sister alone to do the laundry by herself."

Josephine burst into the room. "Oh yes you can. This is what you've always wanted. You can be a real teacher, with a classroom of your own. It would be foolish of you to say no."

She smiled at her sister. "But thanks to the blue petticoat escapade, we have more business than we know what to do with. Did you know, that yesterday I had a request from one of the ladies in town to make her a blue petticoat. She said that Mrs. Goldsmith was awful to her, and she thought it would be fun to wear a blue petticoat the next time they came to town."

Atherton tensed at the mention of Mrs. Goldsmith. "They're coming back?"

Josephine nodded. "She is, according to Mrs. Frost. Her

husband has some business dealings here, or something like that. I'm not prone to gossip, so I didn't press her further."

Atherton nodded slowly. "Interesting. Thank you for telling me what you know. I'll follow up on the information myself."

Then he turned back to Louisa. "It's good of you to think of your sister, but I've spoken with Josephine, asking her if you can be spared. I also sought Tom's blessing before I made this offer to you. As man of the house, I know he takes a vested interest in the two of you and wants to be sure everything you do is respectable. I assured him this job is completely respectable, and as the town's schoolteacher, you would have an esteemed status. There is nothing more precious to us than our children, because they are our future."

She looked over at Josephine. "You knew?"

Josephine nodded. "He wanted it to be a surprise, and he still wasn't sure about the salary."

Tom joined them. "You have to take this job. I know how it broke your heart to be rejected for the position in our old town. And, if you didn't notice, they're paying you the same salary they pay a man."

Atherton chuckled. "Man, woman. It's the same work. And I'd much rather have a lady teaching our town's children."

Louisa smiled. But then she turned to Josephine. "But you need my help."

Josephine shook her head. "I'll manage. Besides, your salary as a schoolteacher is far more than what you would make on your share of the laundry. Even if you just break it down to dollars and cents, taking the position would be give us a better chance at our savings."

Louisa frowned. It was so tempting, but she had so many

questions and feelings of trepidation. "But what if we can't find a ranch near Blessings?"

Tom joined them and put her arm around her. "Don't worry about all the what-ifs. Even future circumstances such as what we discussed earlier. This is your chance for happiness. We don't know what's going to happen in the future. Just a few months ago, we were living on our family's ranch, thinking we were finally saved financially with Father selling the cattle. And then tragedy struck, and it sent us off on this wild adventure."

Josephine nodded. "It's true. I thought my life was over. Everything I loved had been taken from me, and our future looked so bleak. But here we are, in Blessings, and while it isn't the life I wanted, it's still a good life. And I'm surrounded by people I love, and who love me. I thought I'd lost everything, but then I realized I have a wonderful family who has sacrificed so much for me and my animals. And because our faith in each other has never wavered, the Lord has seen fit to provide for us."

Josephine turned and smiled at Atherton. "This man found us a place to live where I could keep my animals. And even though some people think we're strange, we're starting to become part of this community. No one tries to kill my chickens anymore, and we're now producing enough that I'm able to keep some of our neighbors supplied with eggs. I'm getting double what I got for eggs back home and with the extra money you would be bringing in as a teacher, I wouldn't have to worry."

Then Josephine looked at her sisters again. "Since coming to Blessings we've become even closer. I count the two of you as my two greatest blessings in life, even above my animals."

Then she rested her head on Louisa's shoulder. "Please sister, take this job. Follow your dream, because I know that together we will achieve everything we've ever wanted."

Both of her sisters looked at her with such love, that Louisa felt like a fool for even thinking of not taking the job. She turned to Atherton and smiled.

"Of course I will take the job. With such support behind me, how can I say no?"

Atherton smiled. "Then I think we must go outside and greet your future pupils."

She looked over at her sisters, who smiled. Then they went out the front door, where a crowd had gathered. Near the front stood Jonah and his children. Next to them was Celia and her family. Little Isabella and Callie were holding hands, and Louisa was happy to see that Callie had formed a lasting friendship.

"She said yes," Atherton said, smiling broadly. "I do believe that Blessings will have one of the finest schools in the region. And it is because we have found such a fine teacher."

Louisa's cheeks heated at his words. "I hardly think so," she said. "But I thank you for such a fine compliment."

Jonah stepped forward. "It's true. In the few short weeks you worked with my children, they have progressed far more than I could have imagined. It will be my honor to oversee the building of your schoolhouse."

Then he hesitated. "I understand if you don't wish to work with me, but I would like to sit down with you and go over the plans so that the schoolhouse is particularly useful for you."

She had a lot of things to say to him, none of them appropriate for the gathered crowd. So she nodded. "I would be pleased to do so. I'm so touched that you care so much about the quality of the schoolhouse."

Atherton leaned into her. "Just so you know, in the contract we've drawn up for the schoolteacher, it's doesn't prohibit the schoolteacher from being married."

She turned to stare at him. "What on earth are you talking about?"

Atherton grinned. "The missus and I have been talking, and as we looked at sample teacher contracts from other schools, she thought it was a terrible thing for a woman to have to give up teaching if she were to marry."

Louisa gave a small shrug. "I suppose it's because once the children come, she wouldn't be able to teach anymore."

Atherton chuckled. "Perhaps, but I think it is shortsighted on the part of many school boards. If you find a man you wish to marry, you should be allowed to marry him. Who am I to stand in the way of true love?"

Louisa tried not to groan. Atherton was the furthest from wanting to stand in the way of anyone's true love. In fact, based on what she knew of the others in town, he had done everything he could to shove people in that direction.

She glanced over at Jonah. Unfortunately, in this case, Atherton's effort wouldn't bear fruit.

"We'll be working on the schoolhouse on Saturday," Atherton said. "Menfolk, I expect to see you there bright and early. The womenfolk, under my dear Millie's supervision, will have a great lunch spread out for all of us."

He smiled at his wife, who smiled back. Then he continued. "We'll celebrate afterward with a dance."

Everyone gave a small cheer, and the women quickly gathered around Millie to discuss what food they would be bringing.

Atherton wandered off to speak with the men, leaving Louisa alone on the porch steps to stare at Jonah. "It's mighty fine of you to be willing to take on the school project," she said.

He shrugged. "It isn't just me. The whole community is participating. But I meant what I said about wanting to make this special for you. I'm sure you have ideas of how you would like your classroom set up."

She nodded slowly. He held out his arm to her. "I've already begun building some things. I'd like to show them to you if you would be willing to spare the time."

He sounded so hesitant, and Louisa didn't want to let their previous disagreement make things awkward between them.

She nodded. "I got your notes. I only read them today, because I was trying to close off my heart to you. But it didn't work."

She glanced over at her sisters, who nodded at her. She took his arm and let him lead her to a small shed behind his house.

"Why would you want to close your heart off to me? Did I hurt you that deeply?"

Louisa shook her head. "I fear my heart was too deeply engaged with yours."

A cool breeze rushed past them, and she removed her arm from his to pull her shawl tighter around her shoulders.

"The truth is, my feelings for you are deeper than mere friendship. I know it's wrong of me to feel this way, because I know your heart will always belong to your late wife. I wasn't willing to give up being a teacher to be someone's second-best."

They arrived at the shed, and he pulled her close to him. "Is that what you think? That you're second-best?"

She nodded slowly. "I can never be Lily. And that's where your heart is."

He looked at her, studying her face so intently it was almost uncomfortable. But then he pulled her close to him in a warm embrace. "So, you do care."

She inhaled his warm scent, a mixture of sawdust and

pine, of warmth and protection. "I didn't want to burden you with feelings you couldn't return."

He lifted her chin with his hand and stared deep into her eyes. "I thought you couldn't return my feelings. It's true, I loved Lily. But you awoke something different in me, something deep and beautiful. I refused to acknowledge it, because I wouldn't have you give up your dream of teaching. I, too, did not want to be second-best."

He bent and kissed her. His lips were warm and smooth, and the giddy feeling she'd once felt only in the pit of her stomach in those moments of attraction she could not deny, filled her entire body as he drew her close and continued kissing her.

When the kiss ended, he brushed her hair off her face and smiled at her. "A part of me will always love Lily, but that time in my life has passed, and you are my future. I've been speaking to Atherton for quite some time about the town needing a schoolteacher. I'll admit, in a moment of weakness, I confessed my feelings for you, but that I would not act upon them and stand in the way of your dream of becoming a schoolteacher."

He smiled as he looked down upon her again. "I'm sure that is why he put the clause in your contract about not needing to remain unmarried."

She smiled back. "He did make mention of it. But how did you know I would accept? How did you know that I returned your feelings? I thought I had done a very good job of hiding it."

He pulled her close to him again, giving her another warm embrace. "I hoped. If my actions had hurt you that deeply, I had to believe that your feelings were much deeper engaged than you had let on."

He released her from his embrace then gestured toward a bench. "Please, sit. Even though I have every intention of marrying you, I don't wish for someone to come upon us and accuse either of us of impropriety. You are a schoolteacher now, and I wouldn't want anyone getting the wrong idea about you."

His lighthearted tone and smile warmed her heart. Marriage. He wanted to marry her. But he hadn't quite proposed yet.

"In my discussion with Clarissa about her singing dream, she confessed to me that Lily had not been kind to her. Since that time, we've discussed many things, and she's made it clear that I was so blinded by my feelings for Lily that I didn't notice many of her character defects."

He pulled up a chair to sit near her. "After the situation with Callie, I found out many things I did not like about Lily, especially things she was teaching Callie. Lily was always good to me and loving toward our children. But there was a cruel streak within her, and she took it out on a lot of people. I was too in love to notice, just as I loved Callie too much to notice her bad behavior. I've spent a long time in prayer, struggling with my ability to see clearly when it comes to people I loved. After all, you'd spent a great deal of time trying to tell me about Clarissa, and I wouldn't believe you. So what did that mean for my feelings for you?"

There were tears in his eyes, and Louisa reached forward and took his hand. "You love them, that's nothing to be ashamed of."

He squeezed her hand and smiled. "Yes. That is true. But I don't want to make that same mistake again. You have always told me the truth, and I count on you to be a person who will continue to do so, even when it's difficult. Even if you think you're speaking out against someone I love. I think that is what I love about you. Your commitment to honesty and doing the right thing, even when it's hard. I've seen you humble yourself time and again when you've made a mistake, and you graciously forgive others for theirs."

Louisa shook her head. "Please do not make me out to be a saint. I fear in this case, your feelings for me may have blinded you to my faults."

He chuckled. "Well, you did take your time reading my letter."

"I did." She joined him in his laughter. "In case you haven't noticed, I do have a tendency to be stubborn sometimes."

"And I am not without my faults. But I am grateful that you choose to overlook them and love me anyway. I don't know what would've happened had Lily not died. Would I have eventually realized the kind of person she was? I don't like the person she was turning my daughter into, and I'm grateful that you have proven to be a better example to Callie. When she first met Isabella, she picked up some of her old bad habits from the other girl. But I had a long discussion with Isabella's mother, and she was horrified to learn how unkind her daughter had been. We also learned that Isabella once had a schoolteacher who was quite cruel, and she led Callie to believe that now that you were officially a schoolteacher, you would be cruel as well. We explained to her what was wrong with that thinking, but it will take time for the children to learn the difference. But if anyone can be patient with them as they learn, it is you."

Louisa nodded. "It sounds like we all have things we need to learn from."

Jonah took her hands in his. "I was hoping you would say that. I wasted much of my life thinking I had all the answers. But it's become clear to me that there is still much more I need to learn, and I'm hoping that we can learn those lessons together."

He brought her hands to his lips and gave them a gentle kiss. "There are many things a person promises in a marriage vow, but having said them before, what I believe is missing, is the idea of learning and growing together. And though I will promise you all of the things a husband ought to promise his wife, I also want to promise you now, that wherever life takes us, you can be sure of a partner who is not perfect, but will do everything he can to become a better man for you, and support you as you become a better woman."

She smiled at him and pulled her hands away, then patted the empty space next to her. "I will gladly agree to that promise, and so I think we should seal our promise with a kiss."

He smiled at her and shook his head. "I cannot. I asked your brother and sister permission for bringing you here to speak of these things, but we have been gone too long, and I don't wish to disrespect your brother's trust by placing you in a compromising position."

He might not want to, but having enjoyed the deliciousness of his kiss, she wasn't going to take no for an answer when it came to the next one. She got up from her bench and walked over to his chair, then sat in his lap and wrapped her arms around him. "Then I will compromise you," she said, bringing her lips down to his.

He kissed her with a ferocity she hadn't expected. The feelings rising inside her earlier exploded as they kissed. But then he broke the kiss and moved, bringing her off balance enough that he stood and studied her. "There will be plenty of time for that. But let us not get ahead of ourselves, since we are not even officially engaged."

She stared at him. "Whose fault is that? What must we do to become officially engaged? Because now that we have kissed, you must expect that I'm going to want more."

He grinned. "I'm glad for it. And there is so much more. But, not yet."

He bent down to one knee. "Louisa, will you do me the honor of becoming my bride?"

Even though she knew this was coming, tears still sprang to her eyes. "Yes. I will."

He stood and wrapped his arms around her, but before she could entice him into another kiss, she heard a small round of applause.

Louisa turned to see Josephine and Tom, with Atherton and his wife behind them, clapping. "It's about time," Atherton said. "I've never met a more stubborn couple than the two of you. And trust me, I've brought many a couple together."

"Atherton." Millie nudged him. "Don't mind him. He thinks he's something of a matchmaker, and responsible for a great many weddings here in Blessings."

"I am." Atherton said.

Tom and Josephine walked over and threw their arms around the two of them.

"Dear sister," Josephine said. "Your happiness is our happiness."

It felt good, having Jonah's arms around her, followed by her sisters'. But there was still one secret she hadn't shared with him. She pulled away from their embrace. Then went to the shed door and looked around.

Atherton and Millie were walking off, clearly pleased that they had done their work, and no one else was around. She returned to her sisters and now fiancé. "Before we fully agree to join our families, there is one secret we have been keeping from you." She looked over at Tom. "He deserves the truth."

Tom nodded. "He does."

Josephine lit a nearby kerosene lamp, and Louisa pulled the shed door shut, making sure this next part was private.

"We have not been honest with you about our family," Louisa said. "The honest part is how deeply we love you and care for you. But there's something you need to know about Tom."

Tom stepped forward. "I'm a woman. My real name is Thomasina, and I've been disguising myself as a man to protect my sisters."

Jonah stared at Tom, like he was trying to find a woman underneath her manly features.

"I don't understand. How? Your beard looks as real as mine when I have one," Jonah finally said.

The sisters told the story of how they came to Blessings. Of their father's murder, and their deep pain at being refused any assistance because they were women. Tom's voice shook as she explained about her predicament, and her humiliation of being a woman with a beard.

Louisa and Josephine put their arms around Tom as she finished her story. Then Tom said, "I hope you will keep my secret."

Jonah nodded slowly. "It is no greater secret than the one Louisa has been keeping for me."

He explained about Clarissa and her singing.

"I knew something was off." Tom said. "I knew she seemed familiar when I helped her that night the men were harassing her in the saloon. I kept asking her if we knew each other, but she kept telling me no and sitting farther away from me. I assumed she thought that I was being too forward or hassling her like one of the other men. It didn't occur to me that I actually knew her."

A knock sounded at the shed door, Louisa opened it and peered out to find Clarissa and the children standing there. "Come in. You missed Louisa agreeing to marry me."

The children ran to Louisa and threw their arms around her. "We hoped you would say yes," Callie said.

"I prayed for you to be our mother," Nathaniel added.

Jonah patted the children's heads, then gave them a gentle nudge back in Clarissa's direction.

"We have some family secrets that need to be told so that we could all join our families with a clear conscience.

Clarissa looked over at Jonah. "I'm assuming you told them." He nodded. "And they have also revealed a secret to me."

Tom turned and looked at Clarissa. "The night I helped you at the saloon, I was keeping a secret of my own. I am not who you think I am either."

Clarissa's eyes widened as Tom revealed her secret, but then she laughed. "I should have known. You're the nicest man I ever met. After you helped me that night, I remember thinking that you could almost be a woman for your kindness, and here you are, a woman."

They all laughed, and Jonah bent down to his children. "This is a secret you must never tell anyone. Tom will be Uncle Tom, and you must never say anything to the contrary."

The children nodded. It felt good to see how quickly Jonah had become protective of the family secret.

"I'm sorry to hear about your father," Jonah said. "I agree, it does sound like there is a great mystery on our hands. I will do what I can to help you find your father's murderer and bring him to justice."

Clarissa came around and put her arms around Louisa. "And I, as well. It is amazing the conversations you hear in the saloon, things the men confess when they've had too much to drink. I generally don't listen to such things, but I will keep my ears open for anything that might relate to your father's murder."

Once again, Louisa felt strengthened by the bond of family. Not just the unconditional support of her sisters, but of the new family she was gaining as well.

Clarissa gave her another squeeze. "And let me officially welcome you to our family. I was suspicious of you at first because I thought you had your designs on Jonah. But now that I see the great lengths you've gone in order to protect both of your hearts, and that your desire to befriend me was genuine, I cannot think of a happier occasion than bringing you into our family. Lily's attempts to befriend me all turned into ways she could humiliate me. But you are different. You've never shown me anything but genuine kindness and compassion, and I am truly sorry for all of the horrible things I have said and done to you."

Louisa hugged her future sister-in-law. "Thank you for being willing to trust me, and I pray this is just the beginning of our new closeness. I love my sisters dearly, and I'm so grateful to be gaining another."

The children joined them and wrapped their arms around her again. "And we're sorry too," Nathaniel said.

"I'm sorry I was mean to you," Callie said. "I thought, that since you were going to be mean to me, I would be mean first."

Then she looked down at the ground and kicked it. "But you've never been mean to me, and I shouldn't have been scared that you would. You are the nicest person I know, and I hope you will teach me how to be nice like you."

Her heart couldn't possibly be any fuller, but then Clarissa went and opened the door to the shed a bit wider. "We have one more surprise for you."

Jonah held up the lamp. "Take a look around."

The barn was full of furniture. Chairs and benches like what she and Jonah had sat on, and desks. But then, in the corner, along the wall, she saw a row of bookcases.

"I made these for you. The desks, chairs, and benches are for your school room, but the bookcases, those are yours."

He looked at her and smiled. "I remember you saying that the hardest thing for you to leave behind at your old ranch were bookcases full of books. You'd only brought your favorite books, and the ones for teaching, and I know how much pain that caused you. So I built these for you, in hope that over time, you can reestablish your collection."

Louisa ran to the one of the bookcases and touched it. It was beautiful, and along the top Jonah had carved beautiful flowers. "You did this?"

He nodded. "It's my favorite thing to do. No one here has use for such fancy carvings, they mostly need buildings. So, every evening, in my spare time after the children went to bed, I just started making furniture."

He walked over to the largest chair. "This was the first thing I made for you. I remember seeing you, sitting on the stump, with my children carefully balanced up on your lap and your arms around them while you read to them. I thought to myself that it would be nice for you to have a chair, so you could be comfortable while you read. But when I finished, it seemed too personal a gift to give you. So, I thought I would make you a bookcase as a way of saying thank you, but then that seemed too personal."

He pointed at a small heart he had carved among the flowers. "I didn't mean for that to show up, but it did. So, I made another bookcase. Which turned out to be close to the same as the other."

She wrapped her arms around him. "These are the perfect gifts. I will treasure them always. They are exactly what I would've wanted for myself."

He turned and pointed at the school items. "Which is when I decided to start making furniture for the school room. I knew it would only be a matter of time before the schoolhouse was built, and I figured that I couldn't possibly put things that were too personal in basic chairs and benches and desks."

Then he shook his head as he led her to a larger desk. "At least until I started making the teacher's desk."

He pointed to a tiny carving at the back of the desk, where none of the students would be able to see. It had the same heart and flower motif. "As you can see, I wasn't very good at it."

She hugged him tight. "This is fantastic art. It's beautiful. You more than succeeded."

He returned her embrace, then pulled away slightly. "But not in hiding my feelings. I love you, and if I haven't said it enough out loud, at least these pieces can say it for me. But I hope, now that everything is out in the open, we will say it to each other often. I love you."

She stood on tiptoe and kissed him gently. "I love you too."

EPILOGUE

The first weeks of school had been glorious and beautiful. They were more than Louisa could have hoped for. The feel of the chalk in her hands as she wrote on the board, the excitement in the children's faces as they listened to her lessons were all things she'd only experienced in her dreams, yet were even better in reality.

True, not all the children were excited to be there, but she made their learning fun by singing to them, telling stories, and playing games, just as her mother and Miss Estes had done. They'd started with only a handful of pupils, but as word spread to nearby towns about the schoolhouse in Blessings, more families were coming.

As she gave the room one last glance before the parents and students were to arrive for the children's presentations to share what they'd learned so far, she smiled. She never would've imagined that losing out on her dream job would have been the biggest blessing of all. She couldn't imagine the other school being part of such a warm and inviting community. The other families, who'd looked down their noses at her and conspired to keep her from teaching would not have come together to supply the school with so many wonderful things. Not only had her salary been generous, but anytime she needed anything for the classroom, one of the families always mysteriously came through. They had plenty of books, slates, chalk, and even a beautiful map of the world that she'd hung with pride in the center of her classroom.

Jonah entered, carrying a bouquet of flowers, the children trailing behind him. "Are you excited for your big night?"

"I am." She took the flowers from her husband and gently kissed him on the cheek. They'd decided not to delay the wedding, but to marry as soon as the preacher came to town, because apparently, Jonah said she was far too fond of kissing to wait very long.

And he was right.

She was also fond of all the other things that went with the kissing. It was no wonder girls were encouraged not to spend time alone with men.

"Where's Clarissa?" Louisa peered behind the children. She'd taken the night off from singing at the saloon so that she could be here for Louisa's shining night.

Jonah shifted uncomfortably. "She isn't coming."

"What you mean?"

"Do you remember that gentleman who approached her one evening, saying he owned an opera house in San Francisco?"

Louisa nodded. "He seemed very enthusiastic about Clarissa's singing."

"She received a telegram, saying that his star performer had taken ill, and he needed someone to replace her. He begged Clarissa to come, and even sent a hundred dollars as a sign of his sincerity."

Amazing. It was almost too good to be true.

"Are you sure he's on the up and up?" Louisa asked.

Jonah nodded. "I went to Pete, who checked with some of

his contacts, and he said the man is who he says he is. He does own an opera house, one of the nicer ones, and it was reported in a San Francisco newspaper that the primary singer had taken ill. We have no reason to disbelieve the story."

Louisa hoped the unbelievable story was true. She knew it would mean the world to her sister-in-law to have this opportunity.

"Clarissa was terribly sorry to have to miss tonight, but she had to be on the last stagecoach out."

Louisa looked at the clock. It had left thirty minutes ago. "She did the right thing. There will be many other nights where my students perform for their families. This opportunity is one that isn't likely to come again."

He pulled her close. "That's exactly what I told her you'd say."

Before he could kiss her, her sisters bustled into the room. "And what we said as well," Tom said.

"Tom. What are you doing here?" Louisa asked. "Your shift doesn't end for another hour."

Tom smiled. "We were all given the evening off so we could come watch tonight's performance. The manager said it would be good for us to have wholesome entertainment for a change."

Tom chuckled as Josephine shook her head. "I think the more respectable Blessings becomes, the more Atherton and his friends are invested in promoting respectable activities within the town. He truly wants this town to be a source of blessing for all."

As Louisa rested her head on her husband's chest, she couldn't have agreed more. She would've never thought that her dream job as a teacher would happen in a place like this, and she was sure that Clarissa never imagined that her chance to sing in an opera house would have come from a rundown saloon in a tiny town in the middle of nowhere. Blessings came in many forms, which was why this town was a blessing to all.

She turned her gaze back upon her sisters, praying that they, too, would find the blessings that came with seeing the fulfillment of their hearts' desires.

ABOUT THE AUTHOR

A self-professed crazy chicken lady, Danica Favorite loves the adventure of living a creative life. She and her family recently moved in to their dream home in the mountains above Denver, Colorado. Danica loves to explore the depths of human nature and follow people on the journey to happily ever after. Though the journey is often bumpy, those bumps are what refine imperfect characters as they live the life God created them for. Oops, that just spoiled the ending of all of Danica's stories. Then again, getting there is all the fun.

Subscribe to Danica's newsletter for all her latest news: http://eepurl.com/7HCXj

You can connect with Danica on her website: http://www.danicafavorite.com/

Or on Social Media:

BB bookbub.com/authors/danica-favorite

twitter.com/danicafavorite

instagram.com/danicafavorite

facebook.com/DanicaFavoriteAuthor

READER LETTER

Dear Reader,

This past year has been an unexpected, wild ride. So many things that I think are blessings from the Lord end up being more like a curse, and things I think are curses, end up being blessings.

When I was asked to join the Brides of Blessings group, I was excited to continue being able to write historicals, since Love Inspired Historical closed its doors and I'm moving over to Love Inspired to write contemporary. Around that time, I watched The Greatest Showman, and I fell in love with Lettie, the bearded lady. I wanted to write a story about a woman like her finding love.

You're probably thinking I'm crazy right about now, because even though Tom is definitely a bearded lady, she doesn't get her happily ever after in this book. Sorry, I'm kind of a tease, because I'm saving her story for last. It's really special to me, and I'm so excited for you to read it. Yeah, I kind of spoiled it, since now you know Tom will find true love, but as you know from my bio, that's how all my books end. The how is the interesting part. I truly believe that this world needs more hope, and that's something I believe a happy ending always provides.

Which leads me to this story. Knowing I had an unconventional heroine, and two books that had to come first, I thought a lot about the kind of people Tom would have in her life. And again, playing on the idea of oddities from The Greatest Showman, I chose two other odd women, or at least odd for their time, to find love.

Today, we don't see a woman who wants a career or loves books as being strange, but at the time my story is set, Louisa's interests and aspirations wouldn't be considered "normal." And I'll be honest, I'm not normal, either. A lot of women I know aren't normal or aren't the magazine-worthy example of what a woman should be. And that's okay.

Whoever you are, whatever you dream of being, your dream is valuable. YOU are valuable. And you are absolutely worthy of the dreams God put in your heart.

If you need a little encouragement in following your dreams, I've started a group on Facebook called Your Story is Valuable. I'd love to have you join me in a safe place where you can share your dreams.

Or, if you're just a reader, I have a reader's group where you can join me and other people who love my books, and we can chat some more. Danica Favorite Readers Group

The bottom line is that I believe everyone has a meaningful story in our world, and even if your world looks like it's falling apart, my hope and prayer for you, is that you will see a blessing to come from it.

Danica Favorite

ACKNOWLEDGMENTS

Wow! I'm not going to lie, this book was a hard one. Mostly because I wanted to write it SO BAD, and other obligations kept getting in the way. This book was the pretty shiny distracting me from all the things I HAD to do, so it's been hard staying focused the past few months. Especially with all the other crazy life interruptions that got in the way.

I want to thank the other Brides of Blessings authors for not only their contribution to the series, but for inviting me to join them on this crazy ride. More importantly, I am so grateful for their friendship.

Lynn Winchester, Kari Trumbo, Mimi Milan, Heather Blanton, and Dallis Adams, you guys are amazing. Working with you and getting to know you has been a great experience.

JR Tague, thanks for being willing to take on this project to do my copyedits. Especially with the quick turnarounds and my insane schedule.

Evelyne, thanks for making the cover process so painless and giving me something better than I can imagine.

And to my beta readers: Julie, Nethanja, and Marie. You guys are awesome. You will never know how deeply I appreciate your willingness to help out a poor writer with a cold on a deadline. Thank you so much!

To my readers, thank you so much for taking the time to read my books and tell me how much they mean to you. I'm so grateful for you! If you loved this book, I'd love for you to leave a review, so others know.

COMING NEXT IN BRIDES OF BLESSINGS

Where the Snowy Owl Sleeps by Mimi Milan

About the book:

"Healing the heart can be the hardest medicine to make."

Known as "Snowy Owl" amongst her people, Kela Tukumu is less interested in taking a husband than she is in becoming the first medicine woman of her Miwok tribe. Perhaps it has something to do with the fact that she is rather fierce to behold--taller and stronger than all the other women, and even many of the men... or maybe it is simply due to the terrible tragedy she heard all her life--the one that took away her grieving mother before Kela had the chance to even know her. Regardless of the reason, Kela is determined to stay the course. With the influx of new settlers in the territory, her people have suffered much. She has decided it is her responsibility to help them heal. However, doing so may require an alliance with the local town doctor in ways she never imagined.

If Jonathan Edwards could turn back the hands of time, he would have never left his medical practice back east. His wife warned him it would be their undoing and, sure enough, it was. Now he has his wife's blood on his hands, as well as the responsibility of raising their two small children alone. Worse, the town's mayor has charged him with yet another undertaking--unite the townsfolk with the local Miwok tribe. Yet, how can he possibly do so when the very real likelihood exists that it was one of their men who murdered his wife? The last thing he wishes is to betray her memory... an increasingly difficult task when the Miwok's shaman turns out to be the most capable woman he's ever known.

Will sharing their knowledge with one another open a way to healing, or only produce more hurt for both them and their peoples?